# FACES FROM THE PAST

# FACES FROM THE PAST

DAVE TAYLOR

**CITIOFBOOKS, INC.**
3736 Eubank NE Suite A1
Albuquerque, NM 87111-3579
*www.citiofbooks.com*
Hotline: 1 (877) 389-2759
Fax: 1 (505) 930-7244

Ordering Information:
Quantity sales. Special discounts are available on quantity purchases by corporations, associations, and others. For details, contact the publisher at the address above.

Printed in the United States of America.

| ISBN-13: | Softcover | 979-8-89391-174-9 |
| | eBook | 979-8-89391-175-6 |

Library of Congress Control Number: 2024913505

# Table of Contents

This book is dedicated
to my wife, who through
Love and Remembrance,
has been there for me
these past fifty plus years.

# Part I

# A New Adventure

"In all of us there is a hunger, marrow deep, to know our heritage— to know who we are and where we came from. Without this enriching knowledge, there is a hollow yearning. No matter what our attainments in life, there is still a vacuum, an emptiness, and the most disquieting loneliness."

Alex Haley, Roots

# I

Another start to another day. The sun peeking through the drapes catching my eyes, reminding me that I need to fix those drapes or perhaps buy some new ones, anything to stop Mr. Sunshine from hitting my eyes. Buying drapes really was not my thing. That was Helen's, not mine. The empty side of the bed reminds every day of her four year absence. I keep thinking, we were to finish out our years together, but that damn cancer had other plans. Well, you can't live in the past. Now that was a funny thought since I have been working on our family tree these past ten years. It was time to get up.

I struggle to the bathroom and throw some water on my face to help me meet the new day. *I wonder what exciting discoveries I will have among the dead people of the past.* I dressed and make my way down the stairs to the kitchen. Half way down the stairs, I can smell that coffee aroma starting to wake me up. A couple eggs, bacon, hash browns and a couple cups of coffee and I am ready to get started.

My grandson, Peter arrived and greeted his old grandpa. "Morning gramps. How are you feeling?"

"With my hands!", I replied.

"Oh, gramps. I mean how does your head feel? You know….after the fall."

"Yes, I slipped on a rug, hit my head. Had enough sense to call 911 and they took me to the hospital. I was in there for three whole days eating their lovely food. They said I suffered a slight concussion, but after the entire test was done, they said I'm fine, for a sixty-one year old man. That's been two weeks now and I still feel fine. I am thinking about going back to my family tree research. I haven't touched it for over a month."

Peter looked at me, his blue eyes staring. He was 19 years old, slim and handsome. Was he staring at me or at the wall behind me? I could not tell. Still, he was good to his grandpa!

"Any ways", I continued, "I am feeling fine and no more headaches. Time to move on. I don't want to dwell in the past."

Peter came over and gave me a big hug. "I need to leave grandpa. Have to get to work. Maybe you should remove all your throw rugs in the house, so you don't slip again.  I just wanted to make sure you are OK. I can see that you are, so I'm out of here." With those parting words, he left through the front door.

The house was once again quiet. I went back into the kitchen to get one more cup of coffee. Afterwards I went into the room, Helen, my lovely wife for so many years, now singing with the angels, and I had set up for my family research. I reached along the wall and turned on the light. The room was a fairly large room with family pictures hanging all around the room, some dating back to the early 1800's. On one side of the room were two large bookcases containing old collectible books, historical books where family members had lived, maps books showing the layout of a particular city throughout different periods of time. On the east side of the room sat my work area. Large enough to hold my computer and printer, copier and scanner, and still space for me to examine historical papers and pictures. The desk had three drawers on each side. Behind the desk, on the opposite wall, were two file cabinets containing papers regarding family information. This, indeed, was a perfect work area.

I sat down at the desk and picked up a picture of a house with nine people standing and sitting in front of the house. The house was a two story with a covered porch. The picture showed the front of the house and a little bit of the side. As far as the people in the picture, I knew the names of most of the people, from great-great grandfather James Whitney, sitting in the front of the picture, with his wife, Nora, my great-great grandmother; their children, one being my great grandfather Luther Whitney, sitting to the far right. Everyone else was standing. There was one of the nine could not recognize. I remember now, this is where I left off last month. I was trying to track down her name and relationships to the Whitney's in the picture. The mystery woman was medium height with hair in a bun. The dress of all the people was about 1910 or 1915.

*Let me see if there is something in my papers regarding James and Luther Whitney's family that might give me a clue on this mystery woman.* I turn around in my chair and opening the bottom of one of the cabinets, I scan through the many documents regarding the Whitney family. I took out a letter that was given to me years ago. The letter was from my great-great grandfather, James, to his brother, Isaac. Could not read the date exactly. Looked like it was dated April 20, 1910. The letter talked about the photographer he had come out to the farm and take a family picture. Probably that same picture I had in front of me on the desk.

"It was a great time…" the letter read, "…it was a nice spring day. Had a little rain after the picture was taken. There was a total of 9 in the picture. Come out and see us sometime."

"Mother said that Grandpa Higgins is not doing well and expect to pass on in the coming weeks…." The letter went on, but nothing seemed to give me a clue to the mystery woman of the family picture. I closed the cabinet and turned my chair back to the desk.

I stared at the family picture sitting on my desk. I stared at the neighboring paperwork. My eyes stopped at the picture of Helen, sitting on the desk. I looked at her picture for the longest time. "Do you know who these women are?", I said to Helen's picture. *What I need*, I thought, *is a more powerful magnifying glass.* "Helen had one. Where was it?" I thought about it for a while. "I know." I said as I jump out of my chair and made my way into the bedroom and towards Helen's old jewelry box. It was still back in the far reaches of the closet. I still was unable to dispose of certain items belonging to Helen. There it was. I moved some items on the floor so I could get to the box a little bit easier. Finally, I had enough moved away, I was able to open the jewelry box and then open the bottom shelf. There was the magnifying glass; Helen had special ordered years ago. I never know what she used it for, but I was sure glad she had it. This was a beautiful tool. Small red jewels on the handle and around the glass. The glass was about 9 inches in diameter and a 2 inch more powerful magnification at the bottom of the glass. This was going to be perfect for see the details of the family in that picture. I closed the jewelry box back up and made my way back to the research room.

I sat in the chair and pick up the family picture with my left hand and with the magnifying glass in the other, brought both together. As I glared at the picture, going from one face to the other, I called out their names. "Cousin Harry…. Cousin Jack…. Cousin Russell…and you, I was staring at the mystery woman, I really don't know who you are little lady. Then Great-great-Grandfather James, my Great-great grandmother, Nora. My Grandmother Annie and Grandmother's father and mother, Great Grandfather Luther and Great Grandmother Bess." I put the picture and glass down on the table. Rubbing my tired eyes, I wondered if there was something I missed.

Again, I picked up the picture and the glass and started looking at the faces and wardrobes of the individuals. Moving the glass so I could glare through the 10x magnification, I could see the details of their smiles, the cresses in some of their faces. The hair pins of the ladies and the ribbons in the hair of my grandmother, who must have been around the age of 12 at the time of the picture.

As the glass passed over the face of one of my cousins, I thought I could hear women's voices softly in the background.  I stood up quickly, dropping the picture and the glass, and looked nervously around me. I knew I had heard the voices, but from where, I did not know. I looked around the room, went out into the hallway, checked the front room and kitchen, nothing. I went back to the research room and sat back down. That little episode had jarred me. I felt a bit of a headache coming on.

I sat in the chair listening to my surrounding, but only hear peace and quiet. After about five minutes I knew I must have been dreaming the whole situation.

I returned back to the picture in one hand and the glass in the other. Using the 10x magnification again, I started to look at the faces once more. Noting the faces and the names again, passing the image of my grandmother moving towards Luther's…. but wait. I moved the glass back over to my grandmother. Her head was turned towards her father now, before she was staring directly into the lens of the camera. I quickly moved the glass from one member to the other. They all seemed to have their heads slightly changed. I stopped at the woman whose name I did not know. She did seem to move. And then…. there…. I could see that her mouth was moving, like she was talking. I stared at the face, closer and closer, and closer.

*What was happening?* I could see them all starting to talk, I could hear them softly talking. I could see their facial expressions changing. Then I could feel…myself…. being pulled into the picture…closer and closer and closer…. until finally….

"Please hold still! Stop moving around!!"

I was standing up, not at my desk, not even in my house. I was outside. I was staring at the ground and then at my hands. My whole attire had changed. I was dressed in clothing of the 1900's. My eyes start to move up only to see that I was standing behind a man who was hiding underneath a black cloth attached to a big square box mounted on three wooden legs. The man came out of his hiding place, and then moved to the front of the box.

I looked around my environment, noting the rolling hills behind me and flatter land in front of me. I followed the man as he made his way to the front of this box. It wasn't a box; it was a very old camera with the black bellows in the front of the camera. The man's left hand moved to the center of the camera, grasping a cap that was covering the lens. "OK, everyone, hold still for the count of five." His hand came down with the cap and you could hear him, "One…. two…three…four…five." He quickly replaced the cap back on the camera. "That's it. We got it. Great job." As he bothered himself with the dismantling of the camera, I moved around him to see what he had taken a picture of.

The house was a two-story house, with a porch that went around the whole front and side of the house. It was a faded yellow in color; most of the wood was in good shape. My eyes finally fell on the subjects of the photographer's subjects. These were the same nine people that were in the picture I was holding no less than ten minutes ago. They were my cousins, my great-great grandfather James, my Grandmother Annie, my great grandfather and Great Grandmother, and finally the woman I had no name for.

As I slowly walked towards my family, I turned and watched the photographer load his equipment into a 1904 Ford. With a quick crank of the engine, the photographer got into the Ford and shutting the door, wave to everyone as he and his black smog maker backfired down the country road. Bang…bang was all you hear as the car disappeared around the bend in the road.

I again turned my attention to the family before me. They were all dispersing and making their way to the house talking to each other. Great-great grandfather James looked back at me as he was making his journey towards the house. He stopped and turned around, staring at me with his head slightly tilted to the side. "Excuse me sir." He was addressing me. "Didn't you just miss your ride into town with the man with the camera?" He slowly started to make his way towards me. "You were part of the picture taking group, were you not?"

At first, I did not know what to say, so I did the next best thing, I started to stutter. "I…I." I did not want to tell him that I was his Great-great grandson from the future. Did not want to end up in a loony bin for the rest of my life. After all I was still looking like the sixty-one-year-old man I was. Then it came to me. "Sir, I do work for the man who took your picture, but I normally stay a little longer to gather information regarding the family he just took. You know…. names of the people in the picture, what their relationships to each other and any interesting background stories. I sure hope you don't mind?"

James smiled and said, "Not at all, sir. We'd be plum tickled to pass on any information you want. We are about to sit down for our supper, and you are mighty fine welcome to join us." He extended his hand to me, and I seized the opportunity of shaking my great-great grandfather's hand. It was a very rough one that had been seen for many years on this farm. "My name is James. James Whitney." He spoke with authority. "And what do they call you?"

"David. David Harlow." I knew it would be safe to relieve my true name.

"Well, David Harlow, welcome to the Whitney farm." We walked up to the house with his left hand on my shoulder. "David…. that's a good biblical name. Means, beloved." I just knotted my head.

We went onto the porch and entered the front screen door. James spoke loudly, "Mother we're going to have one more guest for supper." The front room looked old and small. Dark green drapes with gold tassels around the edge, the drapes covering the front windows. In front of the drapes were two, well used, chairs, on having a small stool in front of it. There was a small fireplace with a mantel that had two small pieces of painted china on either side and a larger china painted serving dish in the center. On the wall above the fireplace were two charcoal portraits of an older man and woman.

"May I ask who this fine-looking couple would be?" I inquired looking at the features of the charcoal drawings.

"That would be my father and mother. They came over from Ireland around 1835. Landed in New York and then years later, migrated into the Ohio valley."

"What were their names, if you don't mind me asking?" I was still taking in the features of these two people.

"James and Deborah Whitney. They founded this farm back in 1845. The same year I was born." James responded.

"So, you are a junior or better said, James the second." I turned towards James as I was asking the question.

"Yes, James Howard Whitney, the second!" my great-great-grandfather said with pride.

"That's just great! Carrying on the family name." I said. Here were two new persons in my family tree for which I did not know their name before this day. Great-great-great grandfather James, the first, and great-great-great grandmother Deborah. This was fantastic. I continued my look around the room. Across the way from the two chairs was a couch that could seat, maybe, two people. It was framed with beautiful wood carvings and mounted on four beautifully carved wood legs. On the wall hung a picture of Jesus Christ and to the side of the couch was a doorway leading to the dining room. From the front door, you could see down the hallway which leads to the kitchen. Also in the hallway were the stairs where, I presumed, led to the bedrooms.

I followed James down the hallway into the kitchen where James remarked: "Did you hear me, love? We will have another guest for supper." Nora, James's wife, turned her head toward us and smiled. "The more, the merrier." She said with a hot tin of biscuits in hand. James and I turned from the sweet smells of the kitchen and made out way back outside and sat in the chairs located on the porch. We sat and talked about the farm, the weather, and whether we were going to have an early winter this year. *This year…. what year was it?*

"Mr. Whitney, how long have you and Mrs. Whitney been married?" I asked. "You can call me James…going on 33 years." He responded. I knew James and Nora were married in 1877 and with them being married for 33 years, it puts the year that I am in at 1910. "Please call me Dave…so 1910 has been a pretty good year for you and the farm?" I say wanting to confirm the date. "Yes, crops were might good to us this year." He responded, rocking in his chair and looking out at his front lawn. It was a beautiful site. I stood up and walked along the covered porch. There was a red barn in the back of the house with chickens and a couple goats feeding off the ground. Between the barn and the house stood multiple fruit trees, apples, plums, pears, and cherries. Multiple clothe lines were strung from the house and their wash drying itself in the warm, breezy air.

From the house, "Supper's ready.", could be heard. I made my way back around the house to the front porch, where I met up with James once more. "Come, let's give grace for the bountiful we are about to receive."

James said as he extended his arm out, welcoming me into his house. We all gathered in the dining room and Nora pointed out where I should be seated. I sat, placed the napkin on my lap, and looked around the table. Here in my presence were relatives I had only seen in old black and white pictures. Now they were in front of me, in 3D, in full color. I could not stop grinning from ear to ear.

Finally, James laid out his two hands, grabbing the two hands on both sides. We all did likewise. Then we bowed our heads and James said grace, thanking for the food that was before us, blessing the hands that prepared it, asking for a watchful eye on the strangers among us, and thanking Jesus for dying for our sins. With our heads now raised up again, food was being passed around the table. And what a feast; meat loaf, salads, vegetables, mashed potatoes and gravy. As food was being passed around and people were starting to eat, James commented, "This gentleman sitting at our table works with that picture taking man. His name is David Harlow and I believe he can better explain why he is still here." He ended his sentence and was looking straight at me. I took it was my time to speak.

"Hello all, my name is David, as James stated. I stayed after the man with the camera left to get some background information for the picture he took. What I am looking for is your name, your age, and ladies you do not have to give me that information if you don't want." I smiled as I said that. All the ladies smiled as they turned their faces toward the table. "I would as like to get the relationship you are to the Whitney family. Like son to Mr. James Whitney and so on." I pulled out a piece of paper to collect the info. "If you don't mine, James…" I was looking at James. "… could I start with you."

"Well…" He started. "…my name is James Whitney…" Everyone gave out a little chuckle. "…I was born in 1852. This is my farm. I am the head of the household. I've been married to Nora…" He pointed to her. "…these past 33 wonderful years. Is that enough?" He looked at me.

"That was perfect. Exactly what I was looking for. Next." I said as I looked at his wife. "My name is Nora Whitney, wife of James. I'm old enough to know not to be giving my age to a stranger." I smiled as I wrote down the information. "We've had six children, two of them died very early, the other four have married, three of the four have moved away. My son, Luther…" She pointed to him at the table. "…still lives close enough to come join us for supper occasionally." "Thank you very much, Mrs. Whitney." I said as my eye moved onto the mystery woman sitting next to Nora. "Looks like you're next." I said with a smile.

"OK….my name is Elizabeth Bush. I am the daughter to Bess…" This was my Great Grandmother Bess sitting to the right of me. "…my mother works and so during the summer I come down to Grandpa and Grandma Whitney's farm to spend time with them."

"So is Elizabeth Bush your full name?" I asked as I had my face down towards the table writing.

"No, it's Elizabeth Nora Bush."

"Thank you" I said as I wrote down the information into my notepad. This was the missing name in that family picture I was looking at yesterday, or 118 years from today. 118 years. All of these people will be dead. Their families have grown. Their adventures, their ups and downs. Their moves from here, if that is to be, will have taken place. My Grandmother, whom I never met because she died in her last twenties, sitting at the end of the table, maybe being twelve years old. What a great experience all of this was.

The information was now completed. Everyone around the table had been very open in providing information that I already knew, but there were some tidbits that I picked up that was new to me. My Great Grandfather Luther had a scar on his left hand from a run in with a bull on the farm when he was fifteen years old. My grandmother sings at church and has been paid to sing at weddings.

The supper continued for about another hour as I sat there smiling, knowing some of the trial and tribulations these relatives of mine would be going through in the future. After supper was done, the table was cleared, and I insisted in helping wash the dishes. That was an experience in itself. No running water. The water pump was just outside the kitchen door. You brought in the water, boiled it and poured it into a wash basin to do the dish washing. Oh, give me the days when you will be able to turn on the tap to do simple chores! I actually dried the dishes; my Great grandmother and grandmother did the washing.

After the chore of the dishes was complete, I went out on the front porch where I saw James sitting in the porch rocking chair, rocking back and forth, and smoking on a corn-cob pipe. The sweet aroma of the pipe tobacco filled the surrounding area. "Would you care for a pipe full?" James asked as he pointed to the container with his pipe tobacco.

"No, thank you." I replied as I stared out into the field in front of us. "This is a beautiful place you have here." I remarked.

"I like it." He said smiling, taking a draw on his pipe. There was a light rain that started coming down. I held out my hand and saw the drops gather in the valley of my cupped hand. I could feel the rain. It wasn't a cold rain, but rather a warm spring rain, April showers to be bringing those May flowers. "You know, it's about three miles into town and now with this rain, you're going to get mighty wet." I could hear James talking to me as he sat behind me. "Why don't you stay the night, and I will have Luther take you back into town in the morning." I really was hoping he would ask me to stay.

"If it is not too much of an inconvenience, I would very much appreciate it." I said as I turn to meet his face.

"Good then it is agreed." he voiced back. "Let me go tell mother that you will be staying the night." James got up from his rocker and proceeded into the house. A few moments later he returned with a smile and a box. "Mother said it would be no problem at all. You play checkers, don't you?"

I returned the smile and said, "Certainly!" We sat at a small table with two chairs on the porch. The checkers were assembled, James' pipe was filled and lit, and the games began in earnest. After about a half hour, our moves were being supervised by Great Grandfather Luther and my Grandmother Annie. The rain had stopped, and it was starting to get a little dark. My newly found cousin, Elizabeth Bush, had brought out from the house an oil lamp. This provided the necessary light for James to continue to see how well he was beating me. I did not care. Nothing could put me in a bad mood tonight. Not even a beating, and I do mean several beatings, of checkers from my Great-great Grandfather! After the third horrible defeat, James and I turned the checkerboard and the table seating over to Luther and Annie. James and I returned to the rockers on the porch and watched the next challenge being played out. Nora had brought out some iced tea for everyone and it was great just taking in the whole scene.

After an hour, with the cold night air starting to be noticed by everyone, we all made our way in the front room. A fire was started in the fireplace, and we found comfortable sitting around the room. Great Grandfather Luther had left the room but returned shortly carrying a guitar. He brought it out of the case and started strumming it with songs from a long time ago. I sorry, long time for me, not long time for the people gathered in the room! Great Grandfather Luther played, and we all sang. It was great. A few minutes later, Great-great Grandmother Nora, along with Cousin Elizabeth, excused themselves. The next thing you knew, fresh apple pie, topped with freshly made ice cream. The pie was warm, the ice cream was cold. Two opposite sensations meeting together. Each bite of both gives my mouth that wow factor.

By the time it was 8:30, everyone was getting ready to make their way to bed. *Farm time, I forgot!* We all hugged, and I thanked everyone for their time and hospitality. I had a special thanks to Nora and James who openly welcomed me into their home. Elizabeth showed me to my room, and I expressed my thankfulness in meeting her. I closed the door and looked at the spring powered bed. I started to realize that I was tired. It had been a very long and exciting day. I took off my shoes and stripped down to my shorts. I got into bed thinking about the day's events. Then slowly…...slowly….drifted off….to….sleep….

# III

"GRANDPA…. GRANDPA…..WAKE UP……WAKE UP!!" I heard it but could not acknowledge it. Slowly my eyes started to flutter, and my head started to move up. Pieces of paper were coming up with my head, and dribble, from me, had piddled on the table. I reached up and removed the papers. I was slowly waking up. "Grandpa, are you OK?" I was starting to recognize the voice. Peter put his arms around me and helped me straighten up. "Grandpa, you must have fallen asleep here on your desk." Peter said in his caring voice. I finally stood up and surveyed my surroundings.

"Hello Peter, how are you this morning?" I asked in a low quiet voice.

"I'm fine but you look like you had a rough night!" he responded. "Let's get you into the kitchen. I'll get you some coffee and fix you a good breakfast." We both made our way down the hallway and into the kitchen. I sat down at the table while Peter retrieved a cup and filled it with coffee. He placed the cup in front of me. "Drink up. You need it!" He started the process of fixing me breakfast.

After we sat and ate breakfast and talked about his new job, he announced that he had to get to work and told me to take it easy today. I agreed (I lied!) and he took off to work. I sat there for a while thinking over all I had experienced in the last 24 hours. I decided that I needed to be checked out. I got on the phone and called the doctor's office. Yes there was an available time early this morning. I finished off my coffee and got dressed.

The trip to the doctor's office took less than fifteen minutes. Between the waiting room and the examine room, I sat waiting for about thirty minutes. I did not mind. I've known Dr. Jack Stanley for the last 30 plus years. We've played golf together, when he got the chance. He helped me through the death of my wife. He was more than a doctor; he was a friend.

The door of the examine room finally opened. "Well Dave, what brought you into my office today? We didn't have a scheduled golf game, did we?"

"No, no, no. Nothing like that. I needed someone to talk to." I replied.

He sat down on the stool that was close to the chair I was sitting in. "So, what's up?" he asked with a sense of concern.

So, I took a deep breath and started. "We have been good friends for a very long time. And except for a few bogus golf scores, you would consider me truthful, correct?"

He looked at me, wondering where this was heading. He replied, "Yeeess. Go on."

"OK…" I started the story. "Yesterday, I was doing some family research, looking at pictures. As I was taking a closer look at a picture of relatives in front of their farm……I…felt…. I was being pulled into the picture. And before I knew it, I was there. In their front lawn. Standing behind the photographer taking the picture I was just examining. I met…. I really met my relatives in person. I shook their hands; I talked with them. I had supper and played checkers. We all gathered around in the front room and sang songs. I went to sleep in their bed only to wake this morning face down on my desk!" I waited a little while before I continued. "Jack, I am not crazy. I am not making this up to get attention. I've come to you for help or better said, for you to tell me what do you think happened to me?"

Jack looked at his friend. Thinking for a while. *Dave never really lied, except maybe on golf scores, but who doesn't!* "Well Dave. Before today I would say you were not crazy. Now with this story, and you believing it." He looked at Dave, thought a little longer. "Let's get a MRI to rule out any strange things happening in that brain of yours…. just wait here." Jack left the room, leaving me to ponder whether Jack did or did not believe me. About ten minutes later, Jack came back into the examination room. "OK. I've just set you up for the MRI and they will do it now. So, walk across to the street to the MRI Imaging and check yourself in. I will be there after the test to review the results with you."

I thanked Jack and walked across the street to the MRI Imaging building. The personnel in the office were surprised at how quickly my doctor was able to get me in. They thought I must be some kind of VIP. I disrobed and put on the special covering everyone loves to wear. They laid me on the table, and I was just starting to get a nervous. The table moved into position and my thoughts go back to the events of the last 24 hours. The noise of the machine was enough to drive anyone crazy. Finally, it was over. The table moved out and I was allowed to get dressed. I was instructed to wait in the waiting room while the results were analyzed. I must have been waiting out there for about an hour. Finally, Jack came into the room.

"OK Dave, we have gone over the test. We need to talk." He pointed me into an empty office to the side of the waiting room. We sat and Jack looked at the results for another fifteen minutes. "There appears to be nothing abnormal happening in the brain." He paused for what seemed a lifetime. "I would like to send you to a friend of mine. A doctor." Jack started.

"A nut doctor, right?" I asked angrily.

Jack replied in a slow and calming voice. "Look Dave, what you experienced is not normal. Your test shows that you are normal. The next step is to talk to a professional that might be able to shed some light on the situation. You asked me for help, correct?"

"I did"

"So, this is me helping you. I am not sending you to the loony bin, I am sending you to someone who can listen and maybe have some answers......if that doesn't work, THEN WE WILL SEND YOU TO A LOONY BIN." We both started laughing. I knew that Jack was right. This may help me get some answers. Jack started talking again, "His name is Dr. George Books. Let me call him now to see how soon we can get you in to see him. OK?"

"OK"

Jack pulled out his cell phone, got up and started walking around the room. I could not hear everything, but he did say he and I had been friends for many years and this was urgent. They talked on for about five more minutes and finally he clicked off. Jack put the cell back in his pocket and said, "You are all set. He will be expecting you in about two hours. His office is about 45 minutes away but with traffic, it could take longer."

I got up to leave. As I reached the door, Jack said, "Wait a minute. I want you to take a copy of the MRI to Dr. Books." He sat down at the desk in the room; turned to the computer and within a few minutes had produced the copies on a CD. He handed me the disk, shook my hand and wished me well on my travels today. "Remember we have a golf game in three days. Don't get yourself locked up!" He smiled and I smiled as I started heading for the exit door.

It took me an hour to reach the parking lot of Dr. Books. I had another hour before my appointment. Luckily there was a sandwich shop in the medical office building. I stopped in and ordered a cup of coffee. As I sat at a little table in the shop, I began to practice what I was going to say. *Tell him the whole story or just the highlights. Say that I really met my relatives from over 100 years ago or just say I must have been dreaming. I really did not want to miss my golf game with Jack in three days. No, it's best to take my chances that lay out all of the events that happen these last twenty-four hours.* The hour had passed, and it was time to go see the "Nut" doctor.

I took the elevator to the second floor and found the announcement on the door for "Dr. George Books Psychiatrist Ph.D., Psy.D." I entered the office and was met by a lovely young lady behind desk carrying a big smile. She asked my name, my insurance, and time for the appointment. After relaying the information, I took a seat in a very comfortable chair. The wait was no longer than ten minutes. The door marked "Private" open and a middle-aged man stood in the doorway.

Dr. Books stood a little over 6-foot tall, thin build, mustache, nicely groom, a little greying around the temple. He came over to greet me with an extended hand. "Mr. Harlow, I am Dr. Books. Won't you be coming in?" I followed him into his office. The room was nicely done with calming colors, a beautiful oak desk, not too big but a commanding size and a high back chair behind it. There were two chairs facing the desk. Also in the room were a couple chairs facing each other, a couch, and three lamps situated on small tables.

"So should I lay down on the couch while you examine me?" I asked in a fun tone.

"Would you feel more comfortable?"

"Not really?"

"Then why don't we start in the chairs." He pointed to the two chairs that were facing each other. I sat in one, while Dr. Books inhabited the second.

"Dr. Stanley says you have a pretty mean swing of a golf club." Dr. Books started the conversation.

"I can hold my own. You have to with Jack. I think we are pretty well matched." I contributed to the conversation.

"So, Dr. Stanley told me that you had a different experience yesterday. Today he had you through an MRI and everything seems to check out, so why do you tell me about you exciting experience."

I told a deep breath and said, "You are not going to believe me, and I am not nuts!!"

"I am glad you clarified that. Let me make a note......'He is not nuts'… good, so let's go on with the rest of the story." *I was beginning to like this guy!*

"I lost my wife four years ago…" I started my saga. ".… two weeks ago, I injured my head, had a concussion, but everything checked out. Yesterday, I was looking at some family pictures. One particular, taken about 1910, with nine family members in front of their farmhouse." I took a deep breath.

"I'm sorry, Mr. Harlow, would you care for some water?" Dr. Books asked…

"That would be great, and you can call me Dave."

Dr. Books rose and walked over to a mini refrigerator and pulled out two waters. He handed me one, "Here you go Dave."

I thanked me, opened the bottle and took a couple gulps. Dr. Books took his seat and I continued. "I was sitting at my desk looking at the family picture with a magnifying glass, looking at the faces, the clothes, the surroundings. I study it long and hard. Then, I swear, I could start to see their faces slightly turn. I studied them with the 10x part of the magnifier. I swear I could see them talking. I felt myself moving to the edge of the chair. My hands out stretched, reenacting the holding of the magnifier over the picture. Suddenly I could feel my self being pulled into the picture. I could not stop it! I was being sucked into that picture!!"

I told Dr. Books about meeting all my relatives in the picture. Shaking the hands of my Great-great-Grandfather and my Great Grandfather. Talked to the doctor about having supper with the whole family, talking to each one of them. Smiling, laughing, listening to the stories they told me about their lives. "They invited me to spend the night…" I continued,

".. and I did. I fell asleep in their guest bed. When I woke up the next morning, I was again at my desk, my head lying on some papers; I had drooled on the table. After I got up and had some breakfast, I contacted Dr. Stanley, who contacted you."

The doctor's office got very quiet. He continued to make some notes. When he finally looked up, he said, "So how do you feel about all this?" I answered a little rude, "What do you mean, 'How do I feel'?'

"What I mean is, how do you feel about this whole experience. Are you happy it happen? Are you nervous or scared it occurred? Does it bring out deeper feeling you forgot you had?" He asked as his eyes studied my whole being. I thought about the question before answering it.

"Well, I guess I felt happy it happen. I met, or felt I met, relatives I thought I would never meet in this lifetime. I had been researching the names in the picture; I knew all of them accept one; and during the experience, I met the mystery woman. I talked with her and found out her name. I never felt scared. I could not understand what was happening but went along for the ride and it was a wonderful ride. Talking with these folks, laughing, singing songs, having supper discussing lives. It was great. That is how I feel!" It was a long minute before Dr. Books responded.

"Dave, it is my professional opinion that you…" he paused, "…are not crazy, just tired. First off, a crazy person would not seek understanding of the cause of his or her craziness. I know it has been a while since your wife passed away and it sounds like you have been working very hard on you family research. I believe you drove yourself to exhaustion and you think you have experienced this event." I started to protest when he held out hand like a stop sign. "Let me finish. Do I believe it actually happen, no. The laws of physics will not allow me to think that it really occurred. However, you think and feel that the occurrence really did happen. It gave you some peace and closure, in the search for the mystery woman's identity. I would definitely research to verify the name that she told you, really is her name. Maybe you came across her name in a bible or letter. Maybe she really did not tell you about her name in person."

The doctor took a long and deep breath, then continued. "I professionally think that there is some other underline cause for your experience. What it is, I cannot tell just in one sitting. I would encourage you to seek additional help, either through me or one of my many colleges. I think time will reveal the deeper cause of your special event." The doctor stood up and extended his hand. I followed his lead and did the same. As he walked me to the office door, he said, "Take time away from your family research. Go on a long vacation. Just get away. I think you see a whole new change in your outlook." We had reached the door, he opened it and said, "If you feel like it, make another appointment and let's talk. I think it will help."

I thanked him and made my way out of this office. When I reached my car, I just sat in it, looking out the front window. *A nice long vacation. Maybe that is what I need. Just to get away and not think about those faces from the past.* I started the car and headed home.

By the time I did reach home my thoughts were thinking about all the places I could vacation. *I always wanted to go down and stay at the Florida Keys or maybe finally take that trip to Ireland. Helen and I never made it there and it won't be the same without her, but it definitely will give me a break, like the doctor ordered.* I walked through the house in a haze. Finally stopping at the research room. I sat down and look at all the materials I had on the desk. I didn't know if I could just walk away from this just right now. I looked at the picture of the dad with his foot on his first car, a used 1928 Ford. I glance at that family picture that started this whole situation. I saw and looked at the picture of my grandmother standing in her yard next to her brother, my great uncle. I picked up a picture of Times Square probably taken around 1920.

I put the pictures down and then turned my attention to the papers that were among the pictures. Here is the last will of my Great Uncle on my mother's side. Here is the 1900 census showing the Butchers, mother's grandmother family, living in Columbus, Ohio. That letter I looked at before, Great-great Grandfather James' letter to his brother Isaac. I began glancing over the letter. Then I stopped. Read it over again and again and again. *It can't be!*

In the middle of the letter those words, "It was a great time. The weather was great. It was a nice spring day. Had a little rain after the picture was taken. There was a total of 9 in the picture. Come out and see us sometime. "

"It was a little strange, we had a guest at the house, a Mr. Harlow, he stayed the night but left before the sun came up. He said he worked for the picture taking company, but they did not have a Mr. Harlow working for them. At first, I thought was that he must have been a burglar talking his way into the house, but nothing was taken. Just very strange."

"Mother said that Grandpa Higgins is not doing well and expect to pass on in the coming weeks…"

I re-read that paragraph over and over again. I know it was not there before. *Maybe it was there and that is what fueled my dream. But it wasn't a dream. I was there. I met those people. I ate with those people. It was not a dream. This is proof.* I knew I could not take this letter to Dr. Stanley or Dr. Books as proof. They did not read the letter before and so they would not acknowledge that change in the letter. I knew that an extra paragraph had been added into the letter. I somehow had changed history.

I got up from the desk, and starting pacing, looking at the letter, re-reading it over and over. *Enough!* I put the letter back on the desk. *What I experienced must have been real. I need to try it again to see if it was a fluke or not.* I did not want to return to the chair. If it worked again, I did not want to end up having my head down on the desk when I woke up. I decided to try the next trip in my comfortable chair and ottoman in my bedroom, but before that I need to pick a picture. I went to the desk and looked at the pictures I had scathed over the desk. Which one will be my next adventure? The picture of my dad in his suit with his left foot on the running board of his first car. I picked up the picture, picked up the magnifying glass, turned and ran to my bedroom. I planted my bottom in the chair, put my feet on the ottoman, and took the picture in my left hand and the magnifying glass in the right.

Slowly I scanned the picture. Nothing happen. This just was not right. I started to take a deeper look at the picture. Noting the 1928 Ford's grill, then the wheels. I then took the 10x glass within the magnifying glass and started to look at my dad. He was wearing a hat, the back of the hat was turned up, the front turned down. It was fashionable to wear a hat in that fashion during that period of time. Then his suit, stripped, being a black and white picture, I could not tell if it was a dark brown or deep blue, double breasted. He wore a bow tie, look like the same color as his suit. His shoes, two tone, white and brown, wingtips oxfords perforated lace up dress shoes.

I studied his face. A big smile on that rounded face. A sense of happiness. Then there it was…I could see his lips moving, talking, I could almost hear him. I could see his head turn slightly, ever so slightly. Then it started. I could feel…myself…. being pulled into the picture…closer and closer and closer….until finally….

# IV

"Mr. Harlow. Please turn your face a little more towards the camera." The man in front of me was saying. I walked around him and saw he was using a Graflex Century Graphic camera, those used in the newspaper field. He had just snapped a picture of a young man with his left foot on the running boards of a Ford, vintage 1928. "OK, Mr. Harlow. We like taking pictures of our customers after they have purchased their car. We will send you a copy. Why don't you come into the office? We'll get the final papers signed and I will have the garage do some fine tuning on that car's shine." They started making their way into the office. Yes, I recognized Mr. Harlow, he was my dad at a younger age. As those two made their way into the office, I followed a bit behind. As I entered the sales floor for the Ford dealership, I saw a calendar on the wall of one of the offices. October 1927.

In the middle of the sales floor was a duplicate of the car my dad had just purchased. As I started to admire it, one of the salesmen came over to me. "Nice car isn't it. The brand new 1928 Ford Model A. This beauty replaces the Model T. The engine is a water-cooled L-head inline four, 201 cubic inches, providing up to 40 horsepower. The top speed is around 65 miles per hour. Of course, I don't know where you could drive a car with that amount of speed!"

"How much does this new powerful machine cost?" I asked with a straight face.

"They start as low as $365 and can go up as high as $1,200 with the options. The average price, like the one here on the floor, cost $565, with low down and small monthly payments. Are you ready to step up to this latest model?" he asked, looking like he might be making another sale for the month.

"I'm sorry. I am just waiting for a friend who is purchasing one of these hot cars." I responded. The salesman walked away and spied another potential buyer outside among the models displayed. In a flash, he was making his way outside. I went outside and kept my eyes open for my dad to come out to claim his newest trophy. Dad came out with the salesman who had sold him the car. The salesman handled the keys to dad, pointed at the new shiny car in the driveway, shook his hand and wished him well. The salesman turned and went back into the sales floor while dad headed to his new car.

I headed towards his car as he positioned himself behind the wheel. I went around to the passenger side and tapped on the window. He reached over and rolled down the window. "Can I help you?" He asked as he looked at me. Once again, I was in a spot where I had to think fast!

"Congratulations on your brand-new purchase. It's a beauty!" I started out.

"Well thank you. I think it is." He responded.

"My name is…" I did not want to use Harlow. That may create some unwanted questions. "…Mr. Green. David Green." I stuck out my hand to shack his. I continued, "I work for the local newspaper, and I would be very grateful if I could come along with you and get a story for my paper on how it feels to purchase a brand-new car. In fact, to make it more enticing, I'll even buy you lunch!"

"How could I refuse an offer like that? Come on board." He waved his hand welcoming me into his new vehicle. I climbed in and sat closing the door. The car zooms down the road away from the dealership at a top speed of forty miles per hour.

"Boy this new beauty has lots of speed." I commented.

"It sure does, but I'll have to slow it down now, we are entering the town." The town he was referring to have no stop lights, four bars, a hardware store, a city hall, a park in the center with a large gazebo and kids playing around and on the gazebo. The town also had two restaurants. Dad passed the first one and stopped in front of the second one, about a ¼ mile farther.

"This place, I think, has better food." He said.

"Sounds good to me." I replied.

We both exited the car and headed for the front door of the restaurant. Dad paused at the door, turned his head looking back at his brand-new car! "Isn't she a beauty!!?" We continued walking into the restaurant and sat in one of the booths where he could look out and admire the car. We ordered lunch and drank our water.

"So, what exactly are you looking for?" my dad finally asked. I had enjoyed just sitting looking at this twenty something man who would one day marry my mom and produce little old me! I had to return to my newspaper reporter status and start asking questions.

"First off, let me start by asking your age and is this your first car?" I started.

"I turned twenty last June and this is my first new car." He responded.

"So, you just turned twenty, you just bought your first new car, what else is happening in your life?" I explored.

"Well, moved out of the house 3 months ago, started a new job, making very good money. That's why I was able to purchase a brand-new car. I've started to see a girl who works in the same department as I do. She's really sweet!" He answered.

"Sounds like you're on top of the world. So, what are your plans for the future? In five years, in ten years?" I asked.

"Yes, I feel like I am on top of the world. As far as the future goes…. I am an accountant, and I can see myself working my way up to a manager's position. Married, three to four kids. Nice house just outside the town, with a white picket fence, big front and back yard."

"The war is now over." He continued, "Hopefully the last. The depression is on the recovery. Future looks bright and shiny, like my brand-new car!" He said as he looked out the window at his new purchase.

We finished our lunch and went out of the restaurant. We stood there for a while, talking about the weather, the town, and his brand-new car. How I wanted to tell him of his future; three failed marriages, his big fight with one of his children that would leave them never talking again, the death of another child due to pneumonia. I knew I could not tell him. He would never believe me, and I would be locked up as a fruitcake. This was great to see my dad in his youth and his surroundings. To be able to talk with him, exploring what he saw as his future, his hopes, and his dreams. On the other side of the coin, knowing what was in store for him and not being able to communicate that to him, not to be able to warn him. That was disheartening.

I thanked him for his time and his sharing his future plans with a stranger. We shook hands and I saw him get into his brand-new car and head down the road. I stood there for a while not knowing what to do. Then it came to me. I looked around and found the local newspaper office. I walked into the front door and asked the nice little lady behind the desk if I could put in a personal note for a friend. She handed me the form and I started to write: "DH loved traveling back to see your dad. Hope you get this message." I turned the form back over to the lady who said that would be twenty-five cents and that it would show up in tomorrow's advertisement. I walked out of the newspaper office and walked towards the city park in the center of town, smiling all the way!

I sat and watched the kids playing on and around the gazebo, thinking about harsh future they will have with war after war, but will see fantastic developments in health, housing, transportation, and electronics. I must have been there for a while because the sun was starting to dip into the horizon. I walked across the street to the town hotel, paid the $2 for the room and walked up to the second floor to get into the room. It was clean, but little, and no TV! I went down to the lobby and read the local newspaper, to catch up on all the activities around town. I spent about an hour reading some of the interesting local stories.

It was now after 6:00 pm and I went to the restaurant down the street, close to the hotel, to have a bite to eat. Afterwards I walked down to the local theater and watched WINGS. This was a silent movie with a real piano in the theater accompanying the move. Wings was the first movie to win 'Best Picture' in the 1928 Academy Awards. It was great to watch the audience reaction to some of the scenes of the movie. *You ain't seen nothing yet!* I thought.

I stopped at the local bar on the way back to the hotel and had a beer. Afterwards, made my way back to my room and crashed. I fell asleep as soon as my head hit the pillow.

# V

The room was dark, but I could feel myself lying back in my chair with my feet resting on the ottoman. I rubbed my eyes and tried to get use to my surroundings. I push the ottoman away and put my feet flat on the ground. My hands grabbed the arms of the chair and pushed by body into a vertical position. I stood there for a few minutes until I felt a little sturdier.

The message I left myself, I just remembered. I started for the research room, sat in my chair, brought up the internet on the computer and searched for that local newspaper. I brought up the newspaper for that day in October when I was there. Scan each page by page. The message was not there. *Stupid me. I need to look at the next day!* So I brought up the paper for the next day, scanned the entries in the personal section. There it was! 'DH loved traveling back to see your dad. Hope you get this message.'

There you have it! Both travels produced proof I was there. I knew it would be not good showing the proofs to either Dr. Stanley or Dr. Books. They would say the message was there prior and I forgot about only now thinking that the message was brand new. *So why do I have to prove it to anyone? I proved to myself and that is enough! Do I want to go forward with this ability to go into the past? I know it works; I just don't know what to do with it. Deal with it, you idiot! Travel back in time and enjoy it no matter how long this last! How long this phenomenon would last was anyone's guess. Time to sit, relax, and think about my next adventure!*

I moved into the kitchen and started a pot of coffee. While the coffee brewed, I cooked up some bacon, eggs, and toast. Laid it all out in front of me on the table and sat down. The food and drink helped me slow down and calm down from my last experience. An hour or two passed while I finished up my meal and drank the last of the coffee. Where to go next? Next on the adventure agenda was New York City in the twenties.

I decided to take the day and prepare myself for the trip. And when I say prepare myself for the next trip, I mean rest. I've noticed that these trips wore me out. So, taking the advice from my favorite doctor, Dr.ME, I would have rest and plenty of liquids.

About that time, I could hear the front door open. In a minute, Peter's face appeared around the corner. "Hi grandpa, what you up to today?"

"I was thinking about spending the day with you." I responded. Peter smiled as he sat down at the table. "So, what would you like to do today?" Peter asked.

"Why don't we go explore the antique stores downtown?" I suggested.

"As long as I can spend it with you, I'm on board." Peter answered. A great big smile came on my face, and I was as happy as can be.

"Let me finish getting ready and we can head out." I said and hurried to the bathroom to attend to some last-minute deals.

Peter drove as we neared the area where all the antique stores were located. There were three stores on one side of the street and fourth on the other. Lucky for me, Peter has always been interested in antiques, even when he was young. We stepped into the first store, and it took me back in time when I was a youngster. We saw toys I used to play with, furniture that looks like it was taken from my parent's home. There were old comic books, this is where Peter spent a lot of time; and pictures of families and places from long ago, this I was extremely interested in.

If I could travel into my own personal picture collection, I wondered if I could do the same with some of these pictures. I found myself deeply absorbed in World War II pictures, civil war pictures, the ones Mathew Brady had produced. Then there were the family pictures. I didn't know these people, so I looked for pictures where their surroundings were of interest. Peter came over to me and asked how I was doing. I showed him the pictures I had picked out and asked him how he would feel somehow being transported back to those time periods. He looked at the pictures, handed them back to me and said, "Let me think….no TV, no Xbox, no cell phones….and only outhouses! No thank you grandpa. I am perfectly happy living in the time period I live." He held up a photo of a young boy, maybe twelve or thirteen. He wore blue denim and a pair of work boots that looked like they were too big for him... In his hand he held a pitchfork, which was stabbed into a bale of hay. His face was dirty, probably from the hard work he was performing. Behind him was the opening of a barn door and a horse standing in the doorway. "I'm not built to live that life. Yes, I am spoiled, I admit it, but I feel sorry for the youth lost on that boy." Peter handed the photo back to me and started looking at other items in the store.

*I don't blame him. I too enjoy the ease in which we have in our time. I imagine that future generations will look back at our lifestyle and think we had it hard.*

We continued our trip down memory lane as we visited the rest of the antique stores. Afterwards, Peter and I stopped at a local restaurant located next to our last stop. As we sat there in one of the booths of the restaurant, we started to look at the treasures we had gathered during this eventful day. Peter had found some old baseball cards to add to his collection and I had a series of black and white pictures dating from the civil war through the 1940's.

"Why so many pictures of people you don't even know, Grandpa?" Peter asked inquiringly. I did not wish to him my true reason, so I said, "I enjoy picturing myself back in the different past. Looking at what the people wore and the circumstances of the events happening at the time the picture was taken."

We finished our lunch and started walking along the shop's sidewalk. I enjoyed these quiet walks in town with my grandson. Peter broke the silence with an interesting question, "So Grandpa, do you think we will be able to travel back in time to see historical events or even go into the future and see what is in store for mankind, then returning, hoping to correct the errors of the future?"

"That is a very interesting question, Peter…" I started my response, "…I think it would be fascinating to view the past, meet relatives long gone and shake their hands. To be able to view historical events and see them unfold before your eyes. As far as the future, I would not like to see my future and then come back and make a bigger mess. Now maybe going into the future and seeing what the next big Windows or Apple or some other unknown company make it big and then come back to the present and make investments! That would be fun!!" Peter and I laughed as we walked thinking about those future investments!

As Peter drove us back to my house, we talked about what we would do with all the monies we would make with our future knowledge investments. Luckily, neither of us took that thought very seriously and therefore we could laugh about it!!

We got back to my house just as the sun was thinking about saying "Good Night" to the world. I thanked Peter for spending such an enjoyable time with me and waved as he drove off. I entered the house and turned on the lights to the front room. I sat down in my over-stuffed armchair and started to look at the treasures I had brought home. Picture of Abraham Lincoln sitting with General George B. McClellan in a tent, taken by Matthew Brady. Picture of soldiers carefully walking in a bomb torn town in Europe during World War II. Picture of a father and his teen-aged son (supposedly) sitting on a tractor in front of their barn. Probably taken in the 1940's. And finally, a picture of a family circuit in the late 1950's, at some kind of an amusement park. Which one would I try first?

The tiredness and just the feeling of being worn down had left me. These last few hours, spending them with Peter and just taking it easy, restored me. I got myself from the chair and made my way down to my bedroom, bringing my pictures. I laid in my big comfortable chair, put my feet on the ottoman, and found the magnifying glass on the table next to the chair. I picked out the picture of Lincoln and McClellan and placed the other pictures on the floor next to the chair. Using the magnifying glass I started reviewing the picture. The scene was at one of the union encampments. You could see soldiers standing at attention on the sides. The tent was an open style tent with a wood table in the tent and a chair at the table. General McClellan and President Lincoln were seated in chairs at the table just at the opening of the tent. They were looking at each other and not smiling. This was not unusual for pictures taken during this period. McClellan with his moustache and goatee, wearing his union uniform, no hat. You could not see his hands; they were flat on the table. Lincoln, on the other hand, sat straight in his chair with his chimney tall hat sitting to the right of him, on the table, hands in his lap. It looked like there was something in Lincoln's hand. What was it? I used the 10x glass of the magnifying glass to try and get a better look. It looked like it might be…a….

# VI

"Please hold still, gentlemen."

I once again was behind the photographer. This time it was Mathew Brady. As I walked around him to his side, I could see the whole scene live. There was General McClellan sitting in a chair at a table facing the 16th president of the United States, Abraham Lincoln, also sitting. The picture was taken twice. As this process took place I look around in my surrounding. I was at Antietam Maryland, September 1862. I could hear the President and the general talking. Lincoln was saying to McClellan that it was a victory but a failure. The general had the opportunity to follow the confederate soldiers and finally crush Lee's army, thereby finally ending the war. McClellan said he could not follow Lee's army because their number were greater that his and they would have suffered a lot more causalities. Lincoln commented that McClellan had bad information. His (McClellan's) army was 2 times larger than Lee's and the end of the war would have been in his hands.

I stepped away from the conversation. I knew what would happen any ways. I started to take in my surroundings. The air was thick with smells. Urine, sweat, dusk, death. We were on a slight hill. Looking down I could see tents and fire pits strung through the hillside. Soldiers milling around the fire pits talking, laughing, smoking their pipes, with their rifles close at hand. Around the tent, in which the scene was taking place, soldiers stood at attention. You could see columns of soldiers marching in the background, stirring up even more dust.

Mathew finished up with the second shot and walked around the camera, shaking and thanking the gentlemen, subjects of his picture. As he walked back to the camera, I asked if he would like a hand with the camera.

"No. I will take care of the camera, but if you wish to help, you can gather my other equipment and place it in the wagon over there." He pointed to a wagon with four horses stationary about 200 yards from our position. I did what he asked and observed my surroundings. Not all the uniforms were blue; some were a green color. If I remember my history correctly, the green uniforms were the uniform of the sharp shooters.

Mathew Brady had finished with his picture taking and was in his wagon ready to move on. "Excuse me, Mr. Brady. Can get a lift into town?" I asked hoping to save me from walking so far. He answer with a smile on his face, "No problem. Climb on board." I moved myself into a position next to Mathew Brady and held on.

The wagon moved slowly away from the battlefield heading towards the local town. I looked back to take in the historic scene I had just witnessed. Lincoln would relieve McClellan in the next couple weeks and the union army under new general leadership would start to turn the war around, even though it would still continue for a couple more years.

It took about an hour to reach Porterstown. The town was still behind enemy's line but protected by soldier encampments all around. The town was filled with soldiers and not very many civilians. Some of the buildings were damaged due to cannonballs. We stopped at a store front and got out of the wagon. Mathew started to take his camera into the store. I grabbed a couple bags that were left in the wagon and carried them into the store Mathew had gone into.

After dropping off the bags and his thanks to me, I asked if I could stay there for the night. He said yes as long as I helped him print some of the photos he had taken. I told him it was a deal and asked what I could do right then. He had me start to bring the chemicals that would be needed to create the negatives which in turn would be used to print the photo. I worked for about two hours, then Mathew suggested we get dinner. He had an arrangement to eat in the mess hall of one of the encampments. So, we made our way over to the camp just outside the town. We waited in line in the mess hall and then had a seat close by the mess hall tent's opening. The smell in the tent was strong with the soldiers' unwashed bodies sitting around us. It did not seem to bother Mathew or anyone else in the tent; just me.

We sat across from a soldier who looked very tired. "Long day?" I asked as we looked into each other's eyes. "Yes." He paused for what seemed a full minute. Then he continued. "A lot of noise, a lot of death. Useless deaths. Sometimes I don't know why we are here." He whispered this last sentence to me. "We get up early in the morning, take our rifles, and stand in a line, shoulder to shoulder. Then the attack begins. The confederates start running towards us yelling at the top of their lungs. We aim our rifles and when the order is given, we fire! Some of them fall, others make it through and charge us with bayonet and knives. We fight with them hand in hand. I see the blood shot eyes staring back at me. I got lucky today. Do you know what it is like taking your knife and pushing it deep into another man's stomach? His expression of why? Finally, his body forces me down to the ground with him on top. Bleeding. Dead weight upon me. Dead. I pushed the body over to the right of me. My adrenalin kicked in. Two, three more I kill. I never even liked hunting with my dad when I was young. Now I am killing another human being." He finished talking and stared out into nothingness.

I finished eating quickly and then excused myself. I told Mathew I would meet him back at the store and went out of the tent. I start to walk back to the town, passing soldiers marching to and from the front lines. I was on the outskirts of the town, walking by some trees, when I heard a high pitch sound going by my ear. Then one of the branches of the tree I was next to exploded. I was caught by surprise and dropped to the ground. *What the heck just happened?* I stood up and looked at the tree branch and got my answer. A bullet hole could be seen, and I realized someone had been shooting at me. I knew the confederate soldiers also had sharpshooters creating havoc with the union encampments. I hurried into the town and made it to the store that Mathew was using. I had to wait until he showed up before I could go in.

As I sat on a bench in front of his store I started to wonder. What would happen if I was shot and even died? Would I go back to my present or would I die in the past? I guess that I really did not know what to find out. A stranger walked up to me as I was sitting on the bench. He introduced himself as a reporter for a local paper, capturing interesting stories on the war. I told him that I did not have any interesting stories to tell. I did mention that I was able to watch Mathew Brady take a picture of history and that was exciting and when I was walking back into town, a bullet from a sniper's rifle just missed me and landed in the nearby tree. The reporter asked my name and told him it was DH. He thanked me and continued his walk-through town.

Mathew returned to the store in about 15 minutes. After the door was opened, I followed him in. We sat up and talked for about an hour, he told me about the people he had taken pictures of. He had, to me, a great career. Sometimes a little dangerous, but always an adventure. He said he did not know what he would be doing if the camera and the photography had not come into being. We closed up the shop and made our way to bed. He had a small room that contained an even smaller wood bed. My bed was in the supply area. Not too bad. My pillow was a bag of flour and my blanket was a horse blanket. But I was inside from the cold and damp and the danger. It took a little while until my eyes started to flutter and finally close.

# VII

As I opened my eyes, I could see I was back. In my bedroom, in my chair. Like before, this last adventure had taken a lot out of me. The words of that soldier kept repeating over and over in my head and the thought of that bullet coming too close to me. I was a nervous wreck. I sat in the chair for another hour before I ventured to get up. I changed clothes and made my way to the kitchen for coffee and breakfast. After breakfast was completed, I went back to the Family research room and got on the internet. It took a while, but I finally found the news article written during the civil war. The article talked about the day's battles around the Porterstown area. The picture taking of President Lincoln and General McClellan by Mathew Brady. The near hit of a civilian by a confederate sniper as he was walking into town. His name, DH.

These episodes were no longer just dreams, they really did happen. I rested the rest of the day. I did notice that these happenings were very tiring. I knew I could not stop doing it. It was an adventure beyond compare. It took most of the day for the anxiety of yesterday (yesterday of over 100 years ago!!) to move out of my mind. During the day I looked at other old time photographs I had, new ones I had purchased recently, and ones passed down through the family. I was browsing through pictures of New York City around the 1900 time period. The horse drawn carriages, no car traffic or noise, the crowded streets. People on both sides of the street with fruit and vegetable vendors along the way. The men in the felt derby hats and some in the Panama Straw Boater hats, a few in the Lincoln tall hat, cabbies wearing their Cahill and coachman hats. Women in their long dresses and big floppy hats. Some of the hats had flowers while others were don with feathers. 1900….no radios or televisions in the homes. Walking, visiting, window shopping was the thing to do to get out of the house. The bigger cities would be busier than the smaller, less crowded cities. This big city, New York City, would be my next adventure.

I did research on the internet regarding New York City in 1900. What was happening; what to see. The theater district originated in 1900 on 13th Street where The Star theater was located, showing a play called "A Great White Diamond.". I would like to try and see this play or at least walk around the area. This was the beginning of Broadway.

There were 25,000 pushcarts selling food in New York City streets. Telephones outnumber bathtubs in the U.S. Personal hygiene was not at the top of the daily activities. Of course, that was an issue in all of my previous adventures.

I knew I should have waited, but the anticipation of the New York City adventure was just too enticing. I found the magnifying glass and grabbed it with my right hand. With the left hand, I held the photograph of the 1900 view of New York City. My eyes were focusing on the buildings, the horses, the people caught in a moment of time. I looked closer at the people's faces. Nothing was happening. I again studied the faces of the people walking down this big city street, hoping to see their faces move or twitch. Even a little. Nothing. Was the magic gone? Was I done with my adventures? I was exhausted. I laid back in my chair, put the picture and magnifying glass on my lap, and closed my eyes.

Three hours passed when I finally opened my eyes. I felt a little more rested and I sat up in my chair. Again, I picked up the picture and magnifying glass I had placed in my lap. Scanning the picture I could see the lines of the buildings, an image of a person in a nearby window, the pattern of the tie on a man walking towards the camera on the busy street. I used the special magnification to view the faces of the people walking toward the camera. Seeing the detail of the women's hat, the style of the men's facial hair, the hay in the horse's mouth. A couple walking down the street, arms linked, staring at each other, talking. At least it looked like the couple were talking to each other.

And then the movement. It appeared that all the people in the picture were moving closer to the camera. Closer and closer. Then, there, the ever so slight turning of one of the ladies' head turning towards the person she was walking with. I could see her lips start to move….

# VIII

"The man was so rude. He wouldn't even rise when I got up to leave..." The lady's voice trailed off as she was making the statement, passing right by me. I was behind the photographer who was taking the picture of the busy New York City street. The street, like the photograph showed, was crowded with people, horse drawn buggy carriages, and electric cars being utilized by the local taxi company. The horse drawn buggy carriages still dominate the streets and this was proven by the smell of horses and the horses by products! Trolley cars travel north and south, east and west. But I was here, in New York City, in the year 1900.

The photographer picked up his camera and the stand on which the camera was mounted and proceeded to leave the area. With his shot on film, he was ready to move on. "Excuse me", I said as he was about to leave, "what is the name of your photography studio?"

"Davidson Photography, on 32nd avenue". He answered and gave me one of his business cards.

"Thank you very much." I said, "Have a good day." I said with a smile and a tip of my Panama Straw Boater hat.

It was a cool fall-like day. I strolled down the street, looking at the faces as they passed me by, tipping my hat to the ladies. It was one thing to look at a photograph of 1900 New York, it was another to experience the sights and sounds of the city. I stopped and looked in the window of a butcher shop. On the window it was advertising fresh beef at 14 cents per pound, salt beef at 11 cents per pound, a dozen eggs for 18 cents. How I wish I could take a truck load of meats home with me! I continued my walk down the street. Before long the intoxicating aroma of fresh baked breads fills my nostrils.  I could not resist. I walked into the bakery and stared at the breads and pastries.  I bought a loaf of freshly made baguette. So good, so warm, so tasty! I left the bakery, consuming the newly purchase bread and took in the sights of each store I passed. The General store was the best of all. Everything you could imagine was in there. Hats of all kinds, nails for building, flour for cooking, toys for kids, and phones for the household. Wall phones and candlestick phones, different styles and sizes. The store was a wonder.

I left the wonder store and made my way down the street. I came to 13th street and turned to make my way up the street. This was the theatre district. Advertising of the shows being performed. Most were vaudeville shows some were plays that were performed. I stopped and looked at one of the billboards in front of the theater, "A Great White Diamond". This was the Star Theater. Seats were available from $1.50 to $2.00. As I was looking at the prices I started to giggle.

"What do you find so amusing?" a question came to me from behind. I turned and saw this beautiful woman, I judged her to be in her early fifties, dressed in an ivory long dress and same color stylist hat. The dress had buttons down the front starting from the neck. Lace adorned the dress. She wore ivory high button shoes, and she was holding a closed umbrella with her right hand. "Is there something funny in that playbill?" She asked me while her eyes looked at me, so deep, it was as if she could see my very soul. She had the face of an angel, ok maybe not an angel, but her blue eyes and blonde hair, which was in a bun under her hat, just made me speechless. "Well sir?" She was waiting for an answer.

"I'm sorry. I wasn't making fun of the playbill. I was amused at the prices for the show." I spoke and then paused for a minute, "I truly am sorry. My name is David. David Harlow." I extended my hand towards her. She took my hand and slowly shook it.

"My name is Alice. Alice Handferd. Do you live around here?"

"I am afraid I do not. I am just visiting your beautiful town. I come from a small town in Ohio."

"Oh, very well." She said and started to move on.

"Excuse me. I know this is probably very forward, but I am new to your town, and I wonder if you could tell me where the best place to eat might be."

"Well, I normally don't converse with strangers, but you do have a kind face. I would suggest the Park Avenue Hotel. They have an excellent restaurant. "

I gathered up my courage and then…" Would you care to join me for lunch and tell me more about your city? What I should see before I leave."

"You are a little forward, but I am famish and I do not like to eat alone." She said in a soft voice.

I hailed a horse drawn carriage and we made our way to the Park Avenue Hotel for lunch. We stopped in front of the hotel; I exited the carriage and then extended my hand to help Alice down. She interlocked her arm into mine as we walked into the hotel. It was a busy hotel, people coming in and exiting the hotel at a quick pace. The hotel was beautiful with its high ceilings, frescos on all of the walls. The furniture looked very comfortable in a deep red color. We proceeded into the restaurant section of the hotel and were seated by the front window so we could view the people walking by. I ordered a bottle of Chambertin Burgundy for the two of us. Our lunch consisted of Puree of split peas aux croutons soup, a Doucette salad, breaded veal cutlet with peas, and boiled rice. With a finishing touch of an old-fashioned rice pudding for dessert.

We talked the whole time. Her husband died about three years ago, but he left her well taken care of. She voluntaries at the local church and homeless shelters. Her favorite color is blue, like her eyes, and her favorite holiday is Christmas. She attends the theater as much as possible. She loves Marie Studholme and has seen all of her plays. I was not sure who Ms. Studholme actually was; I assumed she was a well-known actress of the time.

She confessed, with tears in her eyes, that this last year had been the hardest for her with her husband gone. I put her hands in mine and lightly squeezed them. "My wife pasted away about four years now." I commented. "It really does not get easier, but you learn to get through it. In time you will be able to handle reminders of your life with your husband and smile about it."

"There are times…" she said, "…when I am sitting in the park, and something will happen there that brings memories of our life together. Then I start to cry, and it feels like I can't stop. I know that it is silly. We had one son who is a comfort to me since his father, my husband, died. But he eventually moved out and start a family of his own."

"My wife and I had one child, a girl, who now is a woman, and she has a son of her own. It all makes me feel old. I always thought that my wife and I would grow old together and now that won't happen." I started choking up after making that last statement.

"I know how you feel. I felt the same way." She said as I think she was holding my hands. Her face seemed to move closer to mine and I could not help but to stare deep into those eyes of blue calm water. Her hair had start of graying along the sides but it did not take away from her beautiful skin, her ears, her nose, her mouth and that smile of hers. We were now staring back and forth, from one to the other.

*Snap out of it. What the hell are you doing! This woman is already dead!*

I smiled at her. "Let's get out of here and go for a walk." I suggested breaking the mood. She nodded and we both rose to leave. I left the 12 dollars to cover the meal and tip. We walked arm in arm out of the restaurant and out of the hotel.

We made our way to Central Park where we strolled arm in arm. Large trees were on both sides of the wide walkway. It was a beautiful day. You could hear the birds chirruping. The blue skies above and the wind ever so gently making its way through the tops of the trees. When we reached the end of the park, Alice said she should be heading home. I asked if I could escort her to her home. She agreed and we walked along the street towards uptown. We reached her home in about an hour. I didn't want that hour to end.

 "When will I see you again?" she asked as we walked through the gate to her modest home and up to the steps. "How often do you make your way into New York?" I ignored her question.

"There is a play at the Star Theater. Would you be interested in seeing the play with me? "I asked, changing the subject. "I can pick you up at 5 o'clock, go out to dinner, and then go to the theatre."

"That would be lovely. See you at 5." she responded as she made her way into her house, shutting the door behind her.

I twisted around and made my way towards the gate to the house. Opened it, turned and took another look at the house. I left, closing the gate. I walked back downtown and the Star Theater and purchased a couple tickets for the play that night. I still had a few hours before I had to pick up Alice, so I walked the streets of New York City. I visited the McSorley's Old Ale House and had a beer at the tavern that was built in 1854. Picked up a newspaper, read and drank my beer. It was a nice couple hours. During that time, however, I still could not stop thinking about Alice. *What was wrong with me? I could not stay, even if I wanted to.* I walked out of the tavern and headed for Alice's home. I stopped a carriage and hired him to take the two of us to dinner and to the theater. I arrived at Alice's house, with our transportation, at 5 o'clock. I went up to the front door to get my date for the evening.

She opened the door and all I could do was stare at her. The long blue dress with sparkles all up and down took my breath away. She stood there like a princess in royal painting. "You look so beautiful." I said. "Ok princess, are you ready?"

She nodded and I presented my arm to escort her out the door. The carriage took us to the restaurant that was located just across from the theatre. We enjoyed a candle lit dinner with a bottle of white wine and Caesar salad. We shared a seafood stew for the entrée and finished with Bellevue Pudding with Brandy sauce. The meal was finished in plenty of time. We strolled across the street to the theatre and proceeded to our seats.

The play was great, and the company was even better. After the play was over, while in the theater's lobby, as we were about to leave, a photographer took our picture. They took Alice's address and promised to mail her the picture. We went outside and I hired a carriage to take us back to Alice's house. On the ride to her house, we stared into each other's eyes, kissed and cuddled. The ride reached its destination, we climbed out and walked up to her front steps. She turned to me and said, "I asked earlier today, and you did not answer me. When will you be back in New York?"

I was hoping she had forgotten the question, but I knew I had to give her an answer. "I do not know when I will be returning to New York. I wish I could tell you, but I can't."

"What is keeping you in Ohio? Your daughter and her son? Could you not relocate to New York and occasionally visit them?"

"It's a little more complicated than that." I responded to her as I pulled her closer to me.

"What complication? Dave, I am starting to have feelings towards you. I know it has only been one day, but I would like to explore these feelings and see where they lead." She said, and I could see a small tear forming in her eyes.

"I too am developing feelings for you, even after the one day." I said as I led her to the bench located just outside her front door. We sat and I reached over and kissed her lips. Those lips, so moist and delicious. I held her in my arms as I quietly spoke, "I am afraid that I will be gone tomorrow and I don't know or can't tell when, or even if, I will be back. I know I should have never let us go this far, but I could not help it. It just happened. I cannot explain to you where I am going. All I know is I cannot take you with me and I cannot be back tomorrow." This was not easy.

"So, take me with you. I don't care where you are going; I just want to be with you." She fired back.

I took her hands. "It is impossible, and I don't want you thinking about me. I want you to be free to meet someone else. To marry and have a love filled life. "

"Oh, I see." She said as she stood up and started towards the front door.

"Wait a minute." I said as I stood up and started towards her. "You do not understand. I care for you an awful lot. But I can't guarantee I will be around. I would not want to stop you from finding true love. You're still young and very beautiful. Please try and understand."

"David, I don't understand. But if you must go, then go. This was a very nice afternoon and I enjoyed it. Please leave now." She spoke these words as she entered her home.

I stood on the front steps, staring at her front door. I turned and made my way to the house's gate. I opened it, turned around to take one last look at the house and closed the gate. I started to head towards the main part of the city. *It's all for the best. Remember this is in the far past. You should not be messing with the past. What were you thinking falling for someone?*

I went back to the Park Avenue Hotel. Requested a room for one night.

"Check out is 10:00 am sir" the desk clerk said as he was handing me the room key.

"No problem. I will probably be gone before that" I retorted back to him. I walked up the two floors and found my room. With a twist of the key in the lock, I was in. The room was tastefully furnished. The chairs and the bed were very comfortable. *Not bad for $3.50 for the night.* Sleep would not come. All I saw was Alice's face. Her eyes, her hair, her lips. *What was I doing? This is stupid. Beyond stupid. Stop this nonsense and go to sleep.* Her face when she went into the house. *I am so sorry, Alice. I never* *want it to go this far!* I could not sleep. I got up, dressed and went down to the hotel's concierge.

"Excuse me sir." I was addressing Mr. Barkley, the concierge. "I wish to put a message into the personal column of your local newspaper. I am leaving first thing in the morning. Can you help me?"

"Of, course I can mister…"

"Sorry, Dave Harlow, room 201."

"Of course I can Mr. Harlow." Mr. Barkley said as he pulls out a piece of blank paper. "Simply write your message down and I will get to the local newspaper. Probably won't come out until the afternoon or evening periodical."

I took the blank paper and picked up a fountain pen that was sitting close to the paper. "Dear Alice, please forgive me. If I could do anything different, I would. Allow yourself to be loved and be cared for. You are a beautiful woman, and I will never forget our special day. DH."

Mr. Barkley counted the number of words. "That will be 75 cents, Mr. Harlow." I put down a five-dollar bill, turned and went back up to my room.

I started to drowse. Alice's face. Her eyes, her hair, her lips…..

# IX

As I opened my eyes, they were wet. I had been crying. I laid in the chair where I started this adventure, breathing deep and thinking about what had just happened. Again, this experience had taken a lot out of me. I closed my eyes for what seemed like an hour. Opening my eyes once again, I got up, dressed and made my way to the kitchen for coffee and breakfast. Pancakes were on the menu for today. I made too many, which was a good thing because Peter stopped by hungry and willing to help me devour the mound of pancakes I had made. *Why did I make so many pancakes? My mind definitely is not on the cooking of these pancakes. That is for sure.* I was thinking of Alice and the day we spent together.

"Earth to grandpa, earth to grandpa." This was coming from Peter. I am glad he did. I had been staring at the wall in front of me. Now my concentration was broken, I was coming back to earth! I smiled and looked at Peter.

"Now arriving from space…Grandpa!" I toyed with Peter. He smiled back as he placed another fork full of pancakes into his mouth. "Sorry Peter, I was kind of lost in my thoughts. What are your plans for today?"

"Work, work and then more work!" Peter responded. "I need to head out after breakfast. I was just checking in to make sure you were ok."

"As well as can be expected."

"So, what are your plans for today, Grandpa?" It was now my turn to spill today's schedule.

"Dishes, laundry, and basic house cleaning. Don't you think the house needs it?"

"Well, just don't work too hard. The house really doesn't look that dirty, Grandpa." Peter commented as he stood up, wiping his mouth with his napkin, which he placed back on the table. He made his way to the front door. "Goodbye Grandpa. Love you." He left as quickly as he came.

The quiet, for some reason, was starting to annoy me. I got up from the table and went over to the CD player, placing the Frank Sinatra album into the machine and pressing play. Frank's music now filled the house. I walked back to the table and finished my coffee. Soon afterwards I moved into the family research room. Started up the computer and started my search for the personal note I left so long ago, yesterday. I found it in the New-York Tribune, dated October 15, 1900.

"Dear Alice, please forgive me. If I could do anything different, I would. Allow yourself to be loved and cared for. You are a beautiful woman, and I will never forget our special day. DH." There it was in all its glory. I then started searching for Alice Handferd. There it was an article dated June 10, 1903. Announcement of Mrs. Alice Handferd marriage to Mr. Glen Black this Saturday, June 13, 1903. She had moved on and found love, or at least another marriage. I then began a search on Mrs. Alice Black and Glen Black.

In the society pages of June 18, 1928, Mr. and Mrs. Glen Black announced their 25th anniversary party was held on Saturday, June 16th.

In the society pages of November 3, 1933; The death of Mrs. Alice Black; age 83; survived by husband, Glen Black and son, Bryan Handferd, from a previous marriage, four grandchildren and one great grandchild.

Alice had lived and died a full life. This brought a smile to my face. It was time to get up and start my work schedule. It took me about four hours for me to do the dishes, the wash, and a little light cleaning around the house. I start to feel like my old self. I left the house, got in my car, and went into town. Walked around the town, stopped and had lunch in the local café. Finally, I stopped at the grocery store to pick food for the next week.

It took about an hour before all the food was put in its proper place at home. With that task completed, I sat and watched television for the rest of the day. Headed to bed around 11 o'clock. I was tired and ready to hit the sack. Tonight, I was going to sleep restfully, I hoped.

The following day came too soon. I was rested. I didn't remember what I dreamed but it must have been good because I woke up with a big smile on my face. I got up and performed my normal task, finishing with a good breakfast and a large cup of coffee. On schedule for today, I have another trip to the store to pick up a couple items I forgot from my last visit and relax again. I was almost feeling like myself, but I wanted to get in one more full day of rest before exploring past places again. I got dressed, picked up my car keys and headed out the door.

On the way to the store my mind was a blank, not thinking of anything. I was watching the road and the environment around me, but that was it. I got to the store, parked the car and walked into the building. It did not take long to pick up and purchase the few items I had forgotten yesterday. As I exited the store, I noticed a woman standing by my car, looking around. As I approached her, she turned around and faced me with a sad face. I stopped in my tracks and just stared at her.

"Are you the owner of this car?" she asked as she pointed to my car. I stood there and just nodded yes. I could do nothing else. "I am afraid that when I was parking my car, I took too short of a turn and dented the side of your car. I did not want to just leave. I wanted to find out whose car it was and give you my insurance information. My insurance will pay for the damage."

"Alice?" I finally said.

"Who?" she responded.

"I'm sorry. You just look like someone I use to know."

"My name is Rebecca. Rebecca Langford. I really am sorry for the damage. I wrote down my name and insurance company along with their phone number and my policy number. Just call them and they will be able to handle the repair process."

It was uncanny. This woman looked to be in her late forties, early fifties. Her eyes, her hair, her nose, her build. Her eyes! It was Alice, but that was impossible. I had to find out more about her. "There doesn't appear to be that much damage. Maybe we can make a deal and you won't have to report it to your insurance company." I finally got the courage to speak. She looked at me with a very suspicious ponderance.

"What kind of a deal are you proposing?" she asked.

"You let me take you out to lunch and we talk. You can even pick the restaurant. Such a deal!" I said, patiently waiting for her reply.

"Just lunch?" she asked as she looked at me with questioning eyes. I nodded yes. "OK, just lunch. And we will forget this whole accident?"

"Agreed." I responded.

"There is a little mom and pop café down the street about a quarter mile."

"That sounds great. I can follow you to the café." I said possible a little too anxious.

We both got into our own vehicles, and I followed her out of the parking lot and down the street. The "Silver Spoon" café was just down the street, and it did look like that mom and pop she talked about. I found a parking space in the back of the café, two spaces from where Rebecca parked her car. As I got out of the car, I eyed the injury to the bumper. There really wasn't that much damage.

We both walked into the café, me following her. The waitress sat us at a table close to the front and with a window with a view. "Order whatever you want. Like I said, lunch will be on me." I wanted her to know that deal was still in place. We both ordered and then sat in silence while I stared at her, and she studied the town outside the window. "OK" I start to speak, bring her attention back to my direction. "Part of the deal is you tell me a little about yourself and your family history." I could detect a smile growing on her beautiful face.

"My name is Rebecca Langford. I live about five miles west of town. I am a widow. My husband was killed in a car accident about four years ago. We have two kids, or rather two adults, six grandkids and one dog named Hector. I am a schoolteacher, fourth grade, at Valley Elementary. I enjoy painting, old movies, and my karate classes…." I think she said that last part for my benefit, "…. I enjoy walking in the park and the occasional eating out at a nice restaurant. I am five-foot four-inches, weight…none of your business, and age…. again, none of your business." I could not help but show my big smile after all this information and non-information was presented to me! "I think that should cover everything. I thank you for lunch." I think she was finished.

"I do thank you for all of the information. It was very entertaining." I responded. "I guess it is now my turn. My name is David Harlow. I too am a widower. Lost my wife about four years ago. One child, or adult, and three grandchildren. I was an engineer for about 35 years, now retired. I spend most of my time looking at old pictures and going over old documents regarding my family tree. I too enjoy old movies and walks in the park. I golf occasionally which will make my arms and legs sore for days." I paused for a moment before continuing on.

"I normally do not pick up strange women and entice them to have lunch with me…" with this, Rebecca smiled and lower her head ever so slightly. "…but you reminded me of a woman, or I should say a picture of a woman taken around the 1900's. Her name was Alice Handferd." With this last statement, Rebecca looked up from her salad and stared at me.

"Alice Handferd was the name of my great-grandmother. Actually, her name was Alice Black. She was Alice Hanferd when she was married to my great-grandfather Hanferd, but after he passed away, she re-married and became Alice Black. My grandfather's last name was Hanferd. The name was passed down to me until I became a Langford when I married my husband. So how do you know about my great-grandmother?"

Do I tell her I met her, and we both fell in love, only to break her heart and leave in the morning? I don't think so. "Like I said I am doing research for my family tree. I came across the wedding announcement and picture of your great-grandmother, Alice Handferd to Glen Black. The picture of your great-grandmother was so stunning, that image stayed with me. When I saw you this morning, I thought the picture in the news had come to life! I just had to find out more about you.  The resemblance between you and your great-grandmother is uncanny."

"I have heard people say that I looked a lot like her." Rebecca remarked.

"You are the spitting image." I added. "Do you have photographs of your great-grandmother?"

"There are pictures my dad had of her in a folder at the house." She explained.

"Could we meet again? I would love to see those pictures." I boldly asked. "How about dinner tonight? I know the deal was just for lunch, but with this new information, and I really would like to see those pictures, we could extend the deal to include dinner tonight. Again, my treat! What do you say?"

There was a pause. Too long of a pause for my comfort. Then finally she spoke, "I don't see why not. I get to choose the restaurant."

"Of course, any restaurant."

"I have always wanted to go to the Edgebrook Inn in Harrisburg. I know it's about ten miles, but I really would like to go there. And after all, I have to dig around the house trying to find that envelope. Say about 7 o'clock?"

"How could I say 'NO' with you having to dig around the house so much? 7 it is. Would you like for me to pick you up?" I asked.

"No that is alright. I will meet you at the restaurant. At 7." She stood up and extended her hand to me. "Thank you again for lunch. I will see you again at the Edgebrook Inn tonight." After a quick shake of the hand, she slipped out of the café's door and headed for her car.

I sat there just watching her movements outside of the café. I got up, paid the bill with tip and headed for the café door. Once in the car, I turned it in the direction of my house. I spent the rest of the day finishing my chores and then getting myself ready for the dinner ahead.

Time seems to fly. It was 7 o'clock as I pulled into the Edgebrook Inn parking lot. When I reached the front door of the restaurant, I could see Rebecca parking her car in the row behind mine. As she got out of her car, her beauty shined the lights illuminating the parking area. She walked up to the front of the restaurant wearing a chiffon blue dress with what looked like a diamond necklace. She definitely was just as beautiful if not more as her great-grandmother. She greeted me with a big smile which put me at ease. I had made reservations, so we were seated right away. She allowed me to order a bottle of wine, for which the Italian Piancornello Rogheto with its deep ruby red color and vibrant fruit and raspberries flavor sounded perfect. The food was ordered, and the night was starting out just right. We even exchanged addresses and phone numbers.

"So did you have an opportunity to find the folder you spoke of earlier today?" I tried not to sound too anxious.

"I found it in the back of the closet. I haven't had a chance to look at the pictures." She took the large envelope out of her purse and opened the metal tab which kept the container closed. About 20 or so pictures emerged from the envelope, all sizes. Some 3 by 4, some 5 by 8, and finally 8 ½ by 11. She started the process of looking at each picture first and then handing it to me to see. Pictures of Alice in her beautiful dresses. Looks like the pictures were taken all around New York City. Some were at parties; some were at the horse races, while others were with unknown people at restaurants. Rebecca really did look like Alice. I would not be able to vote who was the most beautiful. It was definitely a tie. Of course, Rebecca would have an edge since she was in the here and now.

Dinner had arrived. We still had a few more pictures to go through, but we put it aside while we enjoyed the feast that was before us now. For myself, steak and wine. What a combination. Rebecca had a Caesar Salad with shrimp and chicken, along with the wine. After dinner, coffee was served.  I opted for a dinner port. We both felt it was time to return back to the pictures. It was a step back into a time that was forgotten. We had gone through about five photographs when Rebecca stopped and continued to hold onto a particular photograph. She studied it for want seemed like an hour, but finally, while holding the picture, she looked at me. The silence was killing me.

"What is the matter?" I asked as she continued to stare at me. Slowly she turned the photograph in my direction and handed it to me. The photograph was the picture of Alice and me. I remembered. After the play the photographer took our picture and then got Alice's address and promise to mail the print to her. This was awkward.

"Explain." she said with a new look upon her face. That of wonder, anger and contempt. "What type of a game are you pulling? That is, you in the photograph, isn't it? What are you 100, 200 years old? Are you one of those you read about in horror stories where a man cannot die and lives forever and ever?"

I thought I'd answer with confusion in my voice, "I…I don't know what to say. The man in the photograph looks like me, just like the image of your grandmother looks like you." I took a slight pause before continuing, "No, I am not Methuselah, and I am not playing any games. I am just as surprised at this as you are." *Boy, I wish I could show this photograph to my friend Jack and Dr. Books!* "I am sure there is some logical explanation for this. What it is, I have no idea." I took a longer pause before starting up again. "Maybe your great-grandmother met a relative of mine, who looks like me, back then and had their picture taken." I was hoping this would satisfy her.

She took the photograph from me and looked at it, studied it, looking from the photo of me to the real-life me. She seemed to accept it, but then. Do you ever have a period in time where you can pinpoint the exact minute, second when everything changes? This was that moment. Rebecca took the picture and turned it over. Her eyes got wide, her lips, those beautiful lips, tightened. The mood went from great, getting to know you, to who are you and please stay away from me or else I will call the police! She practically threw the photograph at me. Picked up her envelope containing the other pictures; got up, looked at me and said, "Thank you for dinner Dave. Don't contact me again." And she left.

My eyes followed her as she hurriedly made her way to the restaurant door and out, she went. My eyes went from following her to the back of the photograph she flung at me. On the back was stamped, *The Star Theater on Broadway. The play was 'A Great White Diamond'*. Written below the stamp was: *Picture with Dave Harlow, October 22, 1900*. Boy, I did not see that coming! That was a great time with Alice, dinner, play, talking. And then afterwards telling Alice I would not be there for her in the morning. She had the same look as Rebecca just had before Rebecca's grand exit. Wow, loved and lost two women within 48 hours, 100 years apart!

I left the restaurant and headed home. Pull into my driveway, turned off the car and just sat there for the longest time. The house was dark when I entered; I had forgotten to leave a light on. I stubbed in the hallway until I found the light switch. I turned on the other necessary lights and made my way into the kitchen. Brewed a pot of coffee, poured a cup, and then sat down in my leather chair in the front room. It had been a long day.

It was not my intention to sleep in my chair but that is the way it ended. I woke up the next morning a little sore. My leather chair is comfortable but sleeping in it overnight is a little too much.  I got up and made myself a fresh pot of coffee, had a frozen waffle with bananas sliced on top. The first thing on the list today was to take a copy of my birth certificate and a copy of the picture of myself with my mom, circuit 1952. I called a same day delivery service. They were at the house within the hour. I addressed the package to Rebecca's address and presented it to the delivery service. Now I knew Rebecca would get it in a few hours. Maybe, just maybe, she would be convenience that that was not me in the photograph. Of course it was, but I was not about to tell her I simply transported myself back to 1900 and dated her great-grandmother. Actually, I really wanted to tell her, but I knew it would probably make matters worse. Now it was all in Rebecca's hands now. If she did not wish to see me, nothing else could be done.

I worked in the research room cleaning up, relocating books, and reorganizing papers. It took most of the morning and part of the afternoon to finish revamping the room, but it did look better. I sat down in my chair thinking about the next adventure I would like to explore. But did I want to have that type of an adventure? If I was going to be honest with myself, the only adventure I wanted was a continuing adventure with Rebecca. I could not stop thinking about her. Immersing my thoughts on how I could fix it. Maybe I should call. Maybe just show up at her house. Enough, I will just wait to see if she calls. This is going to make for a very long day.

Indeed, it was a long dragged out day. 1 o'clock, 3 o'clock, 5 o'clock and no call. *All is lost. Woo is me!* I looked at myself in the mirror. *Did I really say that? 'Woo is me'? That's pretty sad. Snap out of it.* I went into the bathroom and threw cold water on my face. I made my way into the kitchen and poured myself another cup of coffee and sat at the kitchen table. When I finished, I was resolved! Got up, grabbed my car keys and headed for the car. With a minor detour to the florist, I carried a dozen red roses up the walk to Rebecca's front door. Going for broke. She answered the door without smiling.

"Can we talk?" I started as I was holding those dozen roses. I paused. "I'm afraid these flowers will die if you don't put them in water." I paused again. "Please take the flowers and let's talk. I think we can work this out." I hoped I was not sounding too desperate. She reached out and took the flowers. *Great first step!*

"I was thinking about it. You don't look 118 years old." She said eyeing me.

"I don't feel a day over 61!" I retorted. A smile. I saw a smile break on her face! "I really do not have an answer for the picture of your great-grandmother and that man at the theater."

"A man who looks like you and has the same name?"

This was going to be tricky. "Yes, that man looks similar to me..."

"Exactly like you." She corrected.

"Yes, a man who looks exactly like me and has the same name. Again, I am at a loss. I do not have a definitive answer." I tried to look sincere.

"It still seems impossible. The look, the name."

"What seems impossible is that we are having this conversation. I am not 118 years old. I do not know if I have a relative with the same looks and name from 1900 and I do not even know where the Star Theater on Broadway is or if it ever existed."

I continued, I was on a roll, "I do not have a deep dark secret plan to stalk you. Remember, you hit my car. I was in the store when you hit it. I did not plan for you to hit my car, but you did! Yes, you looked very much like a person I saw in the newspaper achieves and yes, I admit, I wanted to meet you after you approached me. Yes, I wanted to take you out to lunch and then dinner because I am attracted to you." Another moment to pause. "OK I am done. If you want me to leave, I will. Not happily, but I will leave."

Rebecca, holding the dozen roses, looking at me, stepped back, opened the entrance to her home wider. "Come on in." She said.

*YES!*

I entered as I heard her shut the door behind me. She walked past me, and we enter the front room. She points to the fabric bound couch on the far side of the room. "Have a seat, while I put these flowers into a vase." I did as instructed. The mood in the room was changing. Maybe we can both move forward. I hoped.

# X

No losses, no gains. We managed to sidestep the white elephant in the room. The discussion on me being in the picture with Rebecca's great-grandma sort of faded away. We did become very good friends. Very, very good friends. We dated on and off, enjoying each other's company at many events we attended.

I tried to travel again looking at the old pictures but could not. Every time I started to look deep into the picture, Rebecca's face would come into my mind. I would smile, think of her some more and eventually put the picture back on the table in the family tree research room.

Was the traveling a result of my fall and concussion, I don't know. I never saw Dr. Books again and my golfing partner, well we never discussed the matter again. Did I really have the adventures, I did, or at least I felt I did. And what about the little clues I would leave only to find the clues the next day in a newspaper. They were really exciting adventures. Meeting my family from long ago. Seeing first-hand the historic meeting of General McClellan and President Lincoln. Meeting my father when he was younger and the thrill of his first car purchase. And New York City in 1900 and spending that wonderful day with a beautiful woman. Of course, relieving that same sensation of meeting her great-granddaughter. That in itself is worth the journey. Rebecca has been the best thing that has happened to me since the departure of my wife. Was it fate that allowed me to travel back in time only to have fate fulfill my future? I can't answer that.

Where will Rebecca and I end up, don't know at the time. We just keep building the relationship one meeting at a time. I am keeping a special place in my heart for her and maybe she will become a special part of my future.

In the meantime, I am grateful for the venture of interacting with the faces from the past.

# Part II

# Love & Remembrance

"Family means no one gets left behind or forgotten."

—David Ogden Stiers

# PROLOGUE

It has been five years since Dave's wife has died and six months since he has been seeing Rebecca. It appears that a person can have two loves in their life. Rebecca is that second love. It was a rocky start, but life has worked things out and Dave is enjoying every sweet minute of it. He hopes that someday he can share his travel experiences with Rebecca, and she will understand and believe him.

Dave's ability to gaze at a photograph and somehow be pulled into the photo, standing behind the photographer and experiencing the surrounding of the photo image. He can still remember seeing his father at a much younger age, and New York City in the early nineteen hundreds, and even Mathew Brady taking the photograph of President Lincoln and General McClellan. These travels into the past seemed to have stopped, but he's still hoping someday they will start back up again. In the meantime, he continues doing his family research. Sometimes he will break away from the family pictures and gaze upon other photos from the past that he and his grandson Peter acquired during antique shopping.

I

———

The sun had sneaked its way between the curtains in the room. A stream of light hit my face as I opened my eyes and took in a deep breath. "Good morning world." I mumbled as I turned my body away from the beam of light. I knew it was time to get up, my body was telling me it was time to get up, God has sent His stream of light to tell me it was time to get up. Reluctantly I moved the blankets away from my body and moved my feet to the carpeted floor. My body followed this motion and now I was sitting in an upright position on the side of the bed. Slowly, I stood up; and then moving one foot in front of the other I made my way to the bathroom. Standing in front of the bathroom mirror, I could now start my morning routine.

After 45 minutes, a now showered and dressed human being moves with purpose to the kitchen where I will get my first cup of coffee. Luckily the coffee timer is on time, and I grabbed my favorite cup and started to pour my first morning wake up juice. I cooked up some breakfast and seated myself at the breakfast table. Now with a half cup of coffee, some eggs and bacon in my body, I started to feel human again. There was a knock at the front door, and I could hear the door opening.

"Grandpa, are you up?" That was my favorite grandson, actually my only grandson, therefore my favorite, Peter. Peter worked his way down the hallway and found me at the kitchen table with my cup of coffee in hand. He was a tall lean twenty-year-old man with brown hair and brown eyes.

"Morning grandpa, how's your day going so far?"

"I am up, showered, dressed and ready to meet the new day. How about yourself?"

"I need to head off for work, but I just wanted to stop by and check in on you."

"That was nice of you, but I can manage. I am a big boy now, but I do enjoy seeing your smiling face."

"I have a surprise for you tomorrow. So, I will see you early tomorrow, ok?"

"Sounds good to me, I love surprises, can't wait. Have a good day at work today, and don't take any wooden nickels."

"Any what?" Peter looked at me with a quizzical look.

"Never mind, I'll explain later. Go off to work and have a good day."

"Goodbye, grandpa. I love you." Peter said as he hurried out the front door.

"I love you, too." I yelled back as he exited the door. *Peter is such a good boy.*

I smiled and stared down into my coffee cup, not completely sure why. Maybe thinking about my life, my family, and how lucky my life has been. Maybe it's the fact that this good life was interrupted five years ago. It has been five years since my wife passed and I was feeling conflicted. My wife is gone and even though I still have love for her in my heart, there is also a part of my heart that has made room for Rebecca. Can I truly love two women so deeply? Yes, I can. I know Helen would be the first to tell me to move on and find someone special to fill that emptiness

I now felt, and Rebecca is just that someone special. But would Helen really tell me that? My mind goes back and forth with the answer.

I stood up from the table and moved over to the coffee machine, filling my cup up. Then proceeded down the hallway and stopped at the family tree room. Standing there, I glanced around. My eyes stopped at the photograph on the desk of my wife and myself on our honeymoon in Hawaii. I went over to the desk and set myself down, placing my cup of coffee to the right of me. I then picked up the photo with both hands and stared at the picture. It was at the restaurant at the hotel, our first day. We were just talking, enjoying our Hawaiian Margaritas made with orange, lime, pineapple, guava juices, and tequila. Don't forget the tequila and the umbrellas. Helen had insisted on the umbrella! Ah, Helen…looking at the snapshot I started to think how naive we were and with our whole lives in front of us.

I picked up the magnifying glass to look at the detail of the photo. I looked at her eyes, that beautifully formed mouth, and her hands, so petite. I feel like I'm right there, standing in front of her, reaching out to touch her, being drawn into the photo. I quickly put the picture and the magnifying glass down on the desk. I had that feeling again. The same feeling I had felt six months prior when I was looking at those other photographs, of being drawn into the photos. I quickly stood up, pushing my chair away from me.

*Wake up, Dave! It's not happening again. That was a long time ago and it had stopped after I met Rebecca. I had not had another adventure since then, but it did feel so real.*

I took a few minutes and remembered the adventures I had had; the family meeting, seeing President Lincoln, spending time with my dad, and seeing New York City at about the 1900 time period, and then there was the meeting with Alice Handferd, who turned out to be Rebeca's grandmother. Those were indeed great adventures, but they are over, and I must look towards the future, hopefully with Rebecca.

I started to relax, repositioned the chair, and sat once again. *I do love Rebecca, but this time, this space, with that photograph I wanted to think about Helen and all the good times we had starting with that*

*Hawaiian honeymoon.* I once again picked up the photograph and with the magnifying glass in my right hand reexamined the scene in the image. I looked at the guy next to Helen. No beard, no mustache, *I really never liked my looks until I started growing facial hair.* Then it was back to Helen. I wished I could relive those moments once again. Following the outline of Helen's face, I moved the magnifying glass from one side of her face to the other. Her eyes just captured me. It almost looked like they were blinking and her mouth opening ever so slightly. It was like she was calling me, and I felt closer to her. I felt myself being pulled into the photograph.

# II

"One more shot." The man in front of me said as he was holding his camera. I peeked around his shoulder and saw the couple he was taking the photograph of. It was Helen and ME! Well, a much younger me. Again, I look so much better now with the mustache and beard. But Helen, I don't think she changed at all, except for the fact that she was alive and sitting in a booth right in front of me.

*FLASH!*

The bulb from the camera had illuminated the entire booth.

"I will choose the best shot and leave the photograph in your hotel room." The photographer said as he nodded towards the couple and started to exit the restaurant. There I was standing in front of the couple, not knowing what exactly to say. I saw a stack of lei on one of the nearby empty booths. I grabbed a couple and then approached Dave and Helen.

"Aloha." The couple already had multiple lei around their necks, but you can never have too many! "I would like to, again, welcome you to the hotel." I said with a big smile on my face. I carefully placed the lei around David and Helen's necks.

"Well, thank you." David said.

"It's 'Mahalo'. Which means thank you."

"Well then, Mahalo."

"So, do you newlyweds have any plans for the day? I assume you are newlyweds; you both have that glow!" The couple looked at each other and giggled.

"Not right now." David said.

"Perhaps you would allow me to be your personal guide. Show you the wonderful fun times you can have here and around the hotel. My name is..." I hesitated for a moment. "...Jack. Jack Highland."

"Well, that would be great Jack Highland."

"Let me get you a couple more Hawaiian Margaritas while I arrange for our transportation."

"How did you know we were drinking Hawaiian Margaritas?" Helen asked.

"And don't forget the umbrellas, correct?"

"Yes, but how did you know..." I had turned and left the area before Helen had finished her question that would require an answer. I passed the waiter and told him about the couple in the booth, I was pointing to Helen and the younger me, needs another round of Hawaiian Margaritas.

I went to the hotel concierge desk and requested an electric cart able to seat four people. The concierge was very helpful and had one delivered to the front of the hotel. In the meantime, I went back to the restaurant to meet my tourists. David and Helen, who had just finished their drinks and were looking up at me when I arrived.

"Ready to go?" I asked as I stood there in my fancy Hawaiian shirt and a couple leis around my neck.

"We're ready." David said as both of them rose from the table and started to follow me to the hotel entrance and the chariot that would take us all around on our guided tour. As I got into the driver's seat and David and Helen got into the back seat, Helen leaned forward a little.

"Have we met before? You do look familiar." Helen spoke quietly.

"With everyone wearing Hawaiian shirts and leis, everyone looks familiar!" I said as I hit the pedal and the cart took off. Helen jolted back into the seat and into the arms of her new husband, me! We drove for only a few minutes when I pulled over to the curb. To the right of us was a building, Hawaiian style, grass roof and all. I pointed to the building. "This building is the spa area. This is where you can get massages. By the way, they have a special honeymoon massage for two. It's very romantic. There are also showers, whirlpool baths, towels, and wooden lounge chairs where you can stretch out and relax. They play soft music; it's quite peaceful in there. Now behind the building, closer to the beach they have volleyball courts, horseshoe pits, and table tennis."

"Sounds great. I especially like the idea of the massages." This Helen said as she looked into David's eyes. I felt like telling them to 'Get a room', but they already had one.

"Any questions?" I asked as I u-turned the cart and started down the road.

"No." was the reply from them both. I reach the point where we started but then turn right, heading towards the roadway entrance of the hotel. The roadway was lined with palm trees on both sides, very majestic. The road went slightly up so if you were looking behind you, you could see the hotel and all of its surrounding grounds. As I reached the entrance, I pulled the cart over to the right, away from any traffic, so we could turn our glaze to the right and take in the gorgeous view.

"This is truly a fantastic hotel the two of you choose."

"It is beautiful." Helen said, as she took in the view.

"We had always wanted to come to Hawaii and my friend had suggested it." David remarked.

"Bob Roberts." I said as my eyes were looking down, my head slightly nodding.

"Yes, Bob Roberts, but how did you know that?" David asked, and I could feel the eyes of the couple behind me staring at the back of my head. I shouldn't have said that, now what, what was I to say? I turn my body and head toward the back of the cart facing the two, with their quizzical looks penetrating my deepest soul. I had to say something.

"Bob Roberts. He called before the two of you arrived and told the hotel to treat the two of you like a king and queen. He must be some kind of friend. The hotel keeps notes like that in our records so we can respond to our guest."

"Oh…That's something Bob would do." David said, as both, now accepting my explanation, returned their glance to the hotel and its surroundings. *BOY THAT WAS CLOSE!*

"So, are we ready to move on?" I asked.

"Yes." was their combined response.

"Before we go, take a look to your left. If you follow that side road up the hill…" I was pointing so they knew what road I was referring to. "…there is a restaurant that serves traditional Hawaiian meals, very tasty, along with a variety of Hawaiian drinks, with umbrellas." I said the last part looking at Helen. She turned and looked at me smiling.

We moved down the road for a short distance and I pulled over to the right curb. The two looked at me waiting for what I was about to say. I pointed toward the beach area. There was a little village set up with unlit tiki torches set up all around.

"That is the best place to go for a luau. They have the best entertainment and the best food. There is a brochure regarding the luau at the hotel. Call them up and make a reservation. You won't be disappointed. Now over there…" I was pointing about 10 degrees east of the luau area. "…See where that ship is? That ship is called the 'Luau

Sunset' and has the best sunset dinner around. You get to the ship early and they'll take you out. They will serve you a feast fit for a king and queen. Then as the sun sets, you will be on the deck watching the sun slowly sink into the horizon. Again, you can make the reservation through the hotel."

"That's great, Jack. Thanks for the information." David said he looked over the existing view.

"Ready to go?" I asked.

"Yes." They both responded in unison.

"Let's head back to the hotel, there's more to see." I said as I, watching the traffic, made a U-turn with the cart and headed back to the hotel. Finally reaching the hotel roadway entrance, I turned in. We drove past the palm trees on both sides, and the sun above us still shining brightly. When we reached the hotel entrance, I turned our transportation to the right and headed down about a few hundred feet, the beach was always on our left side. I pointed to the left towards the beach area.

"Note that there are pathways all around the hotel to take you wherever you wish to walk. Over there..." I was now pointing to a building decorated the same as their hotel. "...that building has a little market where you can buy cheese, beer, and almost anything you wish to snack on. They also have a couple small shops to buy shoes, shirts, and dresses."

"I like shopping." Helen said excitedly.

"You can say that again!" I mistakenly blurred it out, turning my head towards Helen and getting that look I have seen so many times from her before, letting me know it was something I shouldn't have said. I turned my glance back towards the front, keeping my eyes on the road. We finally reached the destination I wanted to take them to and I made a U-turn so they could look out on their right side. Then I stopped the cart. "Over there..." I was pointing to the right of their view and David and Helen followed my direction. "...there is a little grass hut. See it?

"Yes." They said in unison.

"From that hut, you can get snorkeling equipment. That beach head over there, behind the hut, has the best snorkeling you'll find here. Are you two ready to go snorkeling?" I was looking at them now. They looked at me.

"We are ready!" David said.

"We need our swimming suits", Helen commented. I turned myself facing the front. Pressed on the pedal and we started once again.

"I will drive you back to the hotel lobby. The two of you get your suits on and come back down, I'll wait. Don't worry about towels; they have beach towels at that hut you just saw." I finished my speech as we arrived at the lobby entrance. The two of them hurried off towards their room.

Ten minutes later they were both, once again, back in the back seat of our 'limo' cart. I drove back to the area where the grass hut was and made my famous U-turn.

"Ok you two, go off and have a great time snorkeling. I will be around the area and can take you back when you are done. Take your time."

"Thanks Jack, you're the greatest." David said as the two of them exited the cart and scampered in the direction of the grass hut. I saw them get their equipment and a couple beach towels, and then off to the beachhead where they spread out their towels and headed for the water. I got out of the cart and walked toward the grass hut. I picked up a couple of towels and found an empty lounge chair with an umbrella behind the chair giving just the right amount of shade. I spread out one of the towels and used the second one, rolled up, as a pillow. I sat there on the beach, shaded, and thought about what a great honeymoon it was so long ago.

As I sat there watching my beloved Helen and a thinner me snorkeling in the nearby waters, a waiter came back asking if I wanted a drink. I did not what any alcohol; I wanted to keep a clear head watching these precious moments again, so I ordered a virgin Hawaiian Margarita. Before long the drink arrived, and I charged the drink to David and Helen's room; I'm sure they wouldn't mind! I lowered my hat just enough to block out some of the sunlight. I kept thinking about the wonderful time Helen and I had on that honeymoon. I kept wondering if it was right for me to see these moments again or should I just fall asleep and get out of this dream, or whatever it was. I must have been daydreaming for some time, because…

"Jack." I raised my hat up only to see David and Helen staring at me. "You, OK?" It was David who had awakened me from my daydream.

"Yes, I'm fine, just enjoying the peace and quiet." I responded. "Are you two ready to go back to the hotel?"

"That's why we came over to see you." This was Helen now talking to me. "David and I decided to walk back to the hotel by the pathways."

"Sounds good to me. What are your plans for dinner tonight?" I asked.

"Well… "this was David speaking now, "…we thought we'd try that restaurant at the top of the hill you were talking about. You are welcome to join us."

"Thank you for the invitation, but no. I will, however, drive the two of you up to the restaurant. What time do you want to leave?" David and Helen looked at each other, shaking their heads a little bit.

"Why don't you pick us up at seven tonight?" Helen finally said.

"Seven it is." I said. "I'll see the both of you in front of the lobby at seven." The two walked off along the pathway, holding hands, talking to each other, and dipping their heads towards each other on occasion. I wish I could remember what exactly we were talking about, but it was great to watch the two of them so much in love, and they, we, were.

I had the cart in front of the lobby, at seven that evening, waiting for the couple. Soon afterwards they appeared at the front door of the lobby. David was dressed in shorts and a flowery Hawaiian shirt. Helen appeared at his side in a white summer dress with the same flower design as David. They were, indeed, a matching couple.

"Climb aboard." I said as I sat properly in the front seat.

"Thanks again for taking us, Jack." David said as he sat comfortably in the back seat.

"Jack, can I ask you a personal question?" Helen asked as she leaned forward.

"Go ahead, ask."

"Are you married?" She asked. I pressed on the pedal which sent her flying back into her seat and into the arms of David. "You don't have to answer that if you don't want to." The cart continued rolling up the palm tree lined roadway and towards the main highway.

"I was." I said, keeping my eyes toward the road ahead. "But my wife died about five years ago."

"We are so sorry, Jack." They both said in unison. I turned right onto the main road then shortly turned left which started the cart to ascend up the road to the restaurant. We quickly arrived at the restaurant and the two got out of the cart.

Helen tucked her head back inside the cart. "Jack, we really are sorry. I hope we didn't overstep our bounds."

"Not at all. We'll talk about it later." Helen grabbed the arm of her husband and started up the steps to the restaurant. I got out of the cart and shouted at them.

"Don't forget to ask for a table outside. You have about fifteen minutes before the sun sets. I will be at the bar when you two are ready to leave."

"Thanks Jack." David shouted back. "We'll see you later."

I took the cart and parked it in the designated spot and walked back to the restaurant. I found my way to the bar, found a table outside and when the waitress came by, ordered a virgin Mai Tai along with an order of calamari. The sun started its descent into the ocean blanket. By the time the sun had said good night, my appetizer and drink arrived. It was quite a view from the restaurant. The tiki torches lit all around the restaurant and along the beach below. Hawaii by night, what an atmosphere. Far off I could see David and Helen enjoying the same, with food and drinks, it looked like they were enjoying themselves. I tried to remember the meal with Helen so many years ago, but it was just too many years ago. I could see that I was enjoying the moment even though I could not remember it now. A couple hours went by, and the two honeymooners found me at the table. I looked up at their smiling faces.

"So, are you two ready to head back to the hotel?"

"We are." Helen said as she sat down at my table and the David next to her. "Jack, you're a nice guy. Why haven't you found another 'love of your life'?" I forgot Helen was a part-time match maker, even before we married.

"Well…" I started. "…I just haven't found the right woman. And I would feel a little guilty going out with another woman."

"You know, David and I have talked about this exact issue as we were dating. You never know what the future holds…" I could tell her a couple things! "…and if I would die or David would die, we would expect the other to find another special somebody. It's not like we would forget one another. You see, Jack, love is forever. You can have enough love for your past and your future."

"Jack, if I would die, I definitely would want Helen to find another love. I know she would still love me, but she has so much love that she could love two." This was David, the younger me, speaking now.

"Does that make sense, Jack?" Helen was now looking into my eyes. She was telling me that it's ok to love another when one departs. "You know our vows said to love one another until death do us part. And that is so true." She now grabbed my hand and continued quietly talking, "You have lost someone very dear to you. I can tell, we can tell, you have a lot of love yet to give." She released my hand and I just stared into her face. I first looked at her and then David, then back to Helen. Finally, I spoke.

"So, are you doing anything tomorrow night?" I said lightly looking at Helen.

"Sorry, mister, I'm married!" She said as she held up her hand with her ring staring at me in the face. That same ring was now sitting in a special box in my top dresser drawer.

"Can't blame me for trying?" I said, smiling at both of them. "What do you say we head back to the hotel?"

We all stood up and made our way back to the cart. Small talk and laughs were made as we headed back to the hotel. When we reached the lobby, we all got out of the cart. I went around saying goodbye to the couple.

"Jack, I want to thank you for showing us around the whole day. It was great." David had put out his hand and I shook it. I shook hands with myself, imagine that!

"My pleasure." I released his hand and spoke to both of them, "The two of you have a wonderful honeymoon." It was at that moment that Helen approached me.

"Thank you, Jack. And I hope you do find more love in your life, you deserve it." And then she closed in and kissed my cheek. The two of them then started walking hand in hand into the lobby, occasionally turning back toward me and waving. And then they were gone.

I went into the hotel and dropped off the key to the cart, thanking them for its use. I then walked through the hotel, through the back sliding doors. I walked along the beach and found an empty wooden chair. I sat in the chair and thought about this marvelous day. My wife had just given me her blessing to see other women. The conflict I once had about seeing Rebecca was now gone and I felt a peace come over me. I sat in the chair and thought about the day's events, and I could not help but smile and chuckle. Finally, I closed my eyes and fell asleep.

# III

I woke up, my face planted firmly onto my desk and a couple of photographs stuck to my face. I raised my head and removed the photos, placing them back on the desktop. I got up and made my way to the bathroom, where I splashed cold water on my face to wake myself up. Did yesterday really happen? I wondered. It seemed so real. A smile crossed my face, and I knew deep down, it did really happen, and I got to relive moments with my wife once again. She spoke to me, and I finally was able to get some answers regarding what I need to do about Rebecca.

After toweling my face, brushing my teeth, and combing my hair, I headed to the kitchen. I started my first cup of coffee and decided to go ahead and start making some baby pancakes knowing that my grandson, Peter, would be stopping by. Shortly before the last pancake has been flipped, there was a knock at the door.

"Come on in." I said, knowing who was knocking at the door. I could hear the door opening. Peter shut the front door behind him and strolled into the kitchen. As I looked up from my cooking, I noticed that Peter was dressed in a Civil War Southern uniform.

"What's the occasion Peter? I don't think Halloween is going to be coming around for several months."

"Grandpa, I've joined a Civil War reenactment and I'm in my first battle this afternoon would you like to come. "

"Of course I would love to come. What time is the event happening?"

"It starts about one in the afternoon. I need to be there about twelve to get ready. It's at Fillmore Park. It's a nice big Open Field and you'll have the Southern soldiers on one side and the Northern soldiers on the other and we march towards each other shooting our guns it's quite an event."

"Well count me in!" I said as I sat down at the kitchen table with a plate full of pancakes. Peter joined me as I reached for the first pancake and drank some more of my coffee. "So how long have you been doing this?" I inquired.

"I started about a month ago. I thought it would be fun."

"Well, you sure look authentic. I have some old photographs of Civil War soldiers and you look like you came out of one of those photos."

"That's what I was hoping for, to look like one of those Southern soldiers." Peter said with a smile on his face. The two of them continued to eat their breakfast.

"Ok, I will meet you out on the field at about one." I said. I was looking forward to the event. Peter finished his breakfast and put his dishes in the sink.

"I need to get going grandpa. See you this afternoon." Peter waved as he exited the room followed by the closing of the front door. This sounds like it's going to be a very exciting afternoon. I got up from the table and placed my dishes in the sink. I spent the next few minutes washing and rinsing the breakfast dishes; placing them in the dish rack to dry. I sat down at the breakfast table enjoying one more cup of coffee before starting my day, which would include straightening up the front room.

After my morning tasks were done, I thought I'd better get myself ready to proceed to the park to watch the reenactment. I headed for the bedroom but stopped at the family research room door.

"Where were those photographs of the Civil War soldiers I was talking to Peter about?" I looked on top of the table and on the bookshelf. Next, I looked in the filing cabinet. Under the folder labelled "Civil War" I found what I was looking for. I carried the folder of photographs to the table and sat down. Then I started the process of viewing each photograph one at a time. There were photos of induvial soldiers, both northern and southern; groups of two or more. Scenes from after a battle had taken place. I also came across the photograph of the meeting between President Lincoln and General McClellan. How well I remembered that one. All the photographs show faces with no smiles. Of course, it was common back then not to smile because you had to sit still for a long period of time to have the photograph taken. One of the images caught my eye. It was of a Southern soldier. Looked like maybe he was a private. He was seated on a chair in the woods with an open field behind him. He had that look, like many during that period of time, of frustration and longing. For what, I could not tell. Those eyes, I took the magnifying glass and examined the soldier's face closer; moving the spyglass over each inch of the subject's face; then his hat and jacket; his pants and boots. Then I looked at the soldier's surroundings. I could almost feel myself being pulled into the scene. I remembered this feeling, was it happening again? I could almost touch the rif...

BUZZ...BUZZ...BUZZ

The timer in the other room had gone off. I had set it earlier so as not to forget to go to the park to watch Peter and the Civil War reenactment. I left the photograph on my desk, got up and went into the bathroom to brush my hair one more time and grab a jacket on my way out the door. The park was only two miles away, so it did not take long to get there. I parked my car and picked out a lawn chair that I had in the trunk so I could sit and enjoy the reenactment. I walked towards the open field where I saw other people gathering along the preliminary of the field. I set up my chair and sat down and saw the Southern soldiers were on the west side of the field and the Northern soldiers on the east side. The weather was perfect for the re-enactment, not too hot, and the humidity was low. I saw Peter standing in formation with the rest of the Southern soldiers. Soon we all could hear cannons firing from both sides, with the smoke filling the air. Slowly the Northern soldiers started their move to the west side of the field, guns lowered pointing the way. Southern soldiers were now on the move, heading for the center of the field to meet their nemesis. They too had their guns lowered pointed in towards the Northern soldiers. Suddenly, as the two groups got closer you could see and hear the guns firing. Soldiers would aim and fire their guns and stop and start the process of reloading normally this process would take about 30 seconds if you were good but with a re-enactment, they didn't have to go through all the steps, so it was a lot faster.

The two groups fired more and more shots, with more and more soldiers falling to the ground, pretending to be shot, while the rest continued until they were in front of each other and then they used their guns as battering rams pretending to knock the soldiers down. This process went on for about 10-15 minutes, then the generals, (they looked like generals, or they could have been captains or colonels; I could not tell the difference) on their horses from both sides racing up into the center of the field calling a retreat and the two sides split and went back to their respective sides. Having reached their own sides, the reenactment was over. The Northern and Southern soldiers came together, shaking hands and laughing, walking, and talking about their adventure.

I really wondered how close these reenactments were to the real thing. One thing that the reenactments don't cover is the sweat and the worry or the anxiety of the soldiers looking at the opponent. I cannot imagine being in that position. The rifles or muskets of the Civil War only shot a few hundred yards. But overall, it was fun to watch my grandson and the part he played in the reenactment. He looked like a real Southern soldier.

I met up with Peter about 15 minutes later and we decided to go to a local restaurant to have lunch. We drove separate cars to the restaurant and met at the door, going in together talking about the reenactment.

"I'm sorry, we don't serve Johnny Reb in this restaurant." The host said with a stern looking face. Peter and I just stared at each other.

"I'm just kidding!" The host said with a big smile on his face. "We serve everyone here! I just saw your uniform and thought I'd have some fun with you all. You want a table for two?" We both nodded and the host showed us to our table.

After we were seated, we talked about the actions of the host.

"It's sad to think but that was the mindset shortly before and after the Civil War and for many years afterwards." I said to Peter as we were looking over our menu.

"But the war was over. Shouldn't people move on with their lives?" Peter asked as he put his menu down and was looking at me.

"It was not an easy thing to get over. You are looking at four years of fighting and bloodshed. Brother fighting brother; the north blaming the south for the start of the war and the south blaming the north for all of their losses of life and property. It took years, but the bad feels finally went away." We placed our order and then we started talking about Peter's adventure. Peter said he always enjoyed the Civil War era and found it fascinating, that's one of the reasons why he joined the reenactment.

"As long as you're having fun Peter, that's the important thing." I said, trying to encourage him on.

"I definitely can see me doing this for a long time." Peter said.

The food arrived and I said, "I'm glad you enjoy it. Now let's eat our lunch before it gets cold." We were there in the restaurant for about 30 minutes eating, talking, and enjoying each other's company. Afterwards we both got up and left. Outside of the restaurant we hugged and said our goodbyes. Peter went his way in his own car and I headed back to the house in mine.

I walked in the door of the house and put my jacket on the couch in the front room. Then I headed back to the family tree research room. Peter's Civil War re-enactment had sparked my interest in the Civil War era, and I want to look at the photos I had one more time. I picked up the photograph of the Southern soldier I had left on my desktop. There he was sitting on the chair with the woods behind him and I took up the magnifying glass to look at the detail of his clothes and his surroundings one more time. I could see the stress lines in his face, the worried look, but I also saw sense of love that he had for someone in his life. It showed in his eyes. I moved the magnifying glass over his face looking at the detail of his beard, arm's length in size, ragged, disheveled, and unkempt. As I made my way down to the uniform and the soldier's hands, I could see his tight grip on his beloved rifle. Then I started the examination of the wooded background where he was sitting. I couldn't quite tell what battlefield it was, so I looked closer at his surroundings. I could see the trees and their leaves, and they almost started to move. I started to feel a chill trap in my body. I moved the spyglass over to his face again looking at his hair his mouth his eyes they seem to follow me as I moved around the photo. I studied those eyes and there is something about the eyes. It was happening again, I felt myself being pulled into the photograph.

# IV

Standing behind the photographer taking the photograph of the Southern soldier, I looked around at my surroundings, woods, trees, smoke from extinguished campfires, the smell of blood and death in the air. I moved around to the side of the camera and saw that the soldier I had been looking at in the photo, was now in front of me.

"Hold still now 10 seconds." The photographer said to the soldier as he removed the lens cap on the camera. I could hear him counting to himself, "five, six, seven, eight, nine, ten." Then he replaced the lens cap back on the camera and looked at the soldier. "We are done here. Thank you." The soldier stood up and as he was leaving, I quickly followed him and said.

"Excuse me sir my name is David Harlow. I work for the local paper and would like to ask some questions if you have a moment."

"Sounds fine with me. Do you mind if we just walk over here and sit a spell under this tree? My feet are dog tired."

"Not at all, I need to rest my legs for a while too. So, what is your name soldier?" I asked.

He answered with a smile on his face. "My name is Jimmy Bob Lansford of Charlton, Georgia." Jimmy sat on the ground by the tree with his back against its trunk. I sat at the base of another nearby tree.

"Well Jimmy Lansford of Charlton, Georgia, how long have you been in the camp here?

"Our regiment came here about a week ago. We had heard that the soldiers were moving over Georgia towards Atlanta, and we were assigned to stop them. We met up with the Tennessee volunteers and joined in with them. We settled here just north of Atlanta to stop the northern invasion." Jimmy placed his rifle to the right of him, against the tree. It was a warm, humid day. The position of the sun in the sky told me that it must have been about one o'clock in the afternoon.

"So how did you come about being photographed?" I asked.

"I was just walking around the camp and this feller walked up to me and asked if I would like to have my photograph taken. So, I said sure why not."

"So, Jimmy, are you married, do you have any kids?"

"I've been married for about 4 years now. We have a little girl about three-and-a-half years old. I own a farm just outside of Charlton. Been on that property, I recall, most of my life. Mom and dad are dead now, so I took over the farm and have been working on it ever since. About 3 years ago I was called up to serve with my Southern brothers."

"What are the names of your wife and child?", I asked.

"My wife's name is Samantha and my little girl's name is Abigail."

"You must miss them an awful lot?"

"I sure do. I wish there were a way I could get back and see them. I wrote a letter to my wife." He said as he reached into his pocket and pulled out four pages of paper with writing on it. "I'm hoping to get this to her soon. I also have a necklace with a locket that I've made for Abigail." He had gone into the side pocket of the uniform and pulled out this beautiful heart-shaped locket attached to a string necklace which he held up so I could see it.

"It's beautiful Jimmy. I hope that you'll be able to give it to her soon."

"I'm not sure about that. The fighting is getting pretty heavy nowadays. I just wish I could hide it so no one would take it until after the battle is over and I'd retrieve it then." Jimmy looked at me with his eyes kind of wondering and thinking about what he could do then a big smile came over his face. "I know what I can do." He reached into his pocket pulled out a tobacco tin. It was almost empty, so he took the remaining pieces of tobacco and tucked it into his jacket. Now he had an empty tobacco tin. He took the letter, folded it up and placed both the letter and the locket into the container and closed it up. "Now I need to put it somewhere where I can find it later. Where can I put it?" He said as he looked all around.

"Dig a hole by the base near the tree there…" I pointed to the base of the tree where Jimmy was sitting. "… and then you can always retrieve it later."

"I'm not sure if I will find it again that's the problem."

"Well, let me think…if you were to carve out a heart on the tree with your initials and your wife's initials and have the bottom of the heart point to the bottom of the tree you know exactly where you buried it."

"That's a great idea, I can do that." He stood up and looked at the tree, took out his Bowie knife and started to carve out a heart onto the tree. It was a fairly good-size heart and he had carved in his initials with a little "+" and then his wife's initials. The bottom point of the heart pointed down to the root of the tree. He then took his knife and started to dig a deep hole as deep as he could with the knife. Then he placed the tin which contained the letter and locket inside the hole and covered it by putting dirt on top of it pounding it with his foot to make sure that no one would find it.

"After the battle and you are about to go home you can come to this tree, underneath the heart, dig up the tin and take it home to your wife and daughter."

"Thank you, mister. I really do appreciate your help with this. I feel so much better knowing that it is safe until I can retrieve it." He returned to his sitting position by the tree once again supporting his back. "So, what is your name again, sir?"

"David, David Harlow."

"And how many little ones do you have?"

"Well, my kids are all grow up and I have one grandson."

"A grandson, my oh my. I hope to have grandkids someday. Actually, I want a whole house full of kids of my own. Where is your family staying?"

"They all live on the West Coast of California." I didn't want to tell him, Ohio, that being a Northern state.

"California. I would love to get out there after this stinking war is over."

"You know Jimmy; I have lost all sense of day and time. Do you happen to know what date it is?"

"It's May 17th of course."

"And the Year?"

"Boy you really have lost your sense of time. It's 1864."

"Of course. I've been away from home so long I forgot what the date and year it was."

"I hear you on that. It all seems to blend in together."

"So have you seen much fighting?"

"We've had our share. Those yanks come forward and we fall back. Then we moved forward and the yanks fall back. We have a short break right now. That's why I agreed to have my photograph taken. I'm hoping they will get the photograph of me to my wife. I really do miss her so."

"I'm sure the war will be over soon."

"I hope so. Need to get back to my family and fix up the farm. I'm sure it's seen better days. I don't know how my wife, by herself, can keep things going. I did receive a letter from her about a month ago. She said it was hard but some of the neighbors that are left, come over and gives her a hand."

"Sounds like you have good neighbors."

"Sure do. Why about four years ago I was doing some repairs on my barn and my neighbor, George Saunders, came over and helped. We got the job done in no time. Good old George..." Jimmy paused for a few seconds. "...He was killed about two and half years ago. Two and a half years." Another pause. "Has it been that long? I haven't seen my wife over three years now and my precious little Abigail. Gosh, she must be about four now." He started to stare up into the sky with the beautiful clouds above. I could see the tears starting to come down his face. I wish I could comfort him, but I did not know how. This war would go on for another year. I needed to get Jimmy's mind on something else.

"How far is your farm from Charlton?"

"It's about two miles Northwest. You travel the main road, and then when you come to the fork in the road, go west for about another half a mile."

"How are your comrades in arms treating you?"

"My what?"

"Your fellow soldiers."

"Oh, they're great." He started to stand up. "It's like being with my brothers and cousins." He stood there straight and tall and started pointing to all the tents and campfires happening in the nearby fields. He was now towering over me; I was still sitting on the ground with my legs stretched out. "I didn't know anyone when I first came here; but now we sing and laugh and smoke together. We all watch each other's back."

"What's the first thing you're going to do when you get home?"

"First thing, you ask. I'm going to kiss my wife like I never kissed her before. And then hug my child like there's no" …. I heard a loud whistling noise. I had heard it just as Jimmy was talking. Jimmy had stopped in mid-sentence.  His eyes were glazed over and he just stood there.

"Jimmy, what's wrong?" Jimmy's legs folded and he landed on his knees. His face never changed expression. Finally, his whole body fell forward and over my legs. I could see the back of Jimmy's head. A hole was there with blood gushing out. He had been shot.

"Oh my God!" I said sitting there, still looking at the bullet hole, my eyes wide open.  The Union soldiers must have started another charge. I tried to push Jimmy's body off my legs but for a thin man, he was still very heavy. I looked around quickly but could see nothing or anyone. With all my strength I was able to push Jimmy's body aside. I crouched down close to the roots of the tree I had just been leaning against and surveyed my surroundings. I knew I had to get out of this location.

I started running from tree to tree keeping low to the ground. I would stop for a split second and look back where I had come from. I couldn't see anyone back there. But then again, I heard that whistling sound and the tree I was standing next to would splinter into a million pieces. They were close; I just couldn't see them. I ran as fast as I could using the trees as a cover. First, I'd run to the right and then zig zag to the left. I must have gone 500 yards when I heard that whistling sound again. Then it happened. I was hit on the back of my right shoulder. The force of the bullet hit me like a freight train, and I fell forward, tumbling as I fell, fifty feet down an embankment. Finally ending my fall with my face hitting the ground; leaves from the surrounding area had covered a portion of my body and my right arm fell onto my back. I was sprawled on the ground. My entire back felt like it was on fire. I lay limp on the ground; my eyes closed, and I pretended to be dead. It was easy to pretend, my whole body ached, and I was exhausted. I slowed down my breathing and tried the best I could to relax.

I heard footsteps walking by me; I did not move a muscle. I felt a boot move my leg. I remained limp. I could hear the footsteps moving past me; I had passed the test, I looked dead. I remained in that prone position until night started to cast its blanket upon us. I listened with all my might. I couldn't hear anything. I slowly turned my head to the other side, spitting out leaves that had stuck to my mouth. I got up on one knee and then the other. Finally, bracing myself against a tree I managed to stand up and survey my surroundings. I wasn't sure where I was or which direction to go. I just knew I had to keep moving and try and get help.

Luckily, I was in civilian clothes, a civilian caught up in this war. My left hand automatically went over to my right arm and held it. My whole right side felt numb, and I knew I must have lost a lot of blood. I followed the dirt road I found even though I did not know where it would lead me. I must have walked a mile or two, falling down and getting right back up. The adrenaline in my body was the only thing that was keeping me moving.

I must have walked for about two hours. I was hungry, tired, and hurting like hell. Was this going to be the end? If I died during one of these trips, do I stop existing in my real life, or maybe I will be found dead in my real-life home. I had to stop all these speculations. They weren't doing me any good. Just keep walking, trying to find help.

It must have been another hour but finally I could see campfires in the field just ahead. I didn't know if it was a Southern or Northern encampment, but I didn't care. I was hoping to get help. I made my way into the encampment still holding my right arm. As I passed by the lined-up campfires, I could see they were Southern soldiers.

"Do you have a doctor here?" I yelled out to a couple soldiers who just stared at me. They pointed to a tent situated in the middle of the camp. I managed to walk there, even though it felt like I was dragging my feet all the way. Reaching the tent, an older man sat there smoking his corn cob pipe. He looked up as I approached.

"What happen to you?" He asked between puffs.

"I was shot in the back several hours ago and finally made my way here."

"And you're not dead? Well, we better take a look at you." The man stood up and pointed me into his open tent. "Lieutenant…" The man shouted to a solider standing next to his tent. "…help this man with his jacket." The Lieutenant, a younger man, came over and helped me remove my jacket. He then proceeded to remove my white shirt. The shirt was covered with dirt and mud and blood on the back side. The older man, I assumed he was the doctor, began to look me over.

"Come sit on the table." The wood table, which was located in his tent, had seen many bodies. There were dried blood stains around the edges, and it smelt like death. I sat there on the edge of the table with my feet dangling. The doctor looked at the front of my right shoulder then the back.

"The bullet did not go through. It's still in there and we must get it out. Lay down on your stomach."

I turned my body, with the help of a couple soldiers, and finally was lying on my stomach, my eyes fixated on the back of the tent. I could hear movement all around me, but I could not tell what exactly was happening. The doctor had brought a bottle of what looked like water in front of my face.

"I'm afraid I am out of Ether and Chloroform at this time, so I suggest that you take a swig of this moonshine. And let me tell you, it's the best moonshine this side of the Mississippi river." I took the bottle and took a big gulp. It tasted like furniture polish and burned all the way down. "Now, you're going to have to be a brave." The doctor removed the bottle and saw him take a big gulp himself before returning it back to his desk. The Lieutenant came around to the front of the table and placed a wood twig in my mouth.

"Here, bite down on this. It will help." Two other soldiers came to hold me down on the table. I bit down and prayed to God I would survive this ordeal. I could feel the doctor's hand on my back. He made an incision with some kind of sharp instrument. I bit down hard on the twig, screaming inside my brain. Then the doctor took some kind of instrument or tool in his hands.

"This might hurt a little bit." I heard him say, knowing he had probably used that same line on all his patients, and I knew it was going to hurt more than just a little bit! The tool started probing in my back. I bit down on the twig. It finally reached its goal and grabbed the ball that was lodged in my shoulder. I screamed more in my brain biting harder down on the twig, nearly breaking it in two. The doctor pulled out the ball and threw it on the dirt floor.

"There, that takes care of the bullet, but I can't seem to stop the bleeding." After a few minutes, which seemed like hours to me, I could see the doctor out of the corner of my eye. He went to his desk in this tent and found his army issue knife.

"Find this man another stick for his mouth." The doctor said to his corporal as he went out of his tent and found a nearby campfire. The corporal had just inserted another wood stick in my mouth as the doctor reentered the tent. "You three, hold him down.", the doctor said in a commanding voice. The doctor picked up the bottle of moonshine from his desk and made his way back to my position. He poured some of the moonshine on my shoulder which made its way into my open wound and then took the tip of the red-hot knife and applied it to my wound. The stick dropped out of my mouth as I screamed the loudest, I have ever screamed. The doctor then repositioned the knife and again reapplied the blade to my bare, bleeding wound. Again, I screamed and screamed and screamed until I passed out.

# V

I woke up, face down on the floor next to my own desk. Photographs that were on the desktop last night were now strung-out around the floor with me. I was tired, weak, and my shoulder hurt like hell. I used the chair to help me get up. After a couple tries, I was able to stand on my own two feet. I felt dizzy and my shoulder hurt as if it had been hit by a sledgehammer. I staggered down the hallway, holding my shoulder, through my bedroom, and into my bathroom. I removed my shirt to look at my shoulder. It looked perfectly normal, but it really did hurt. I showered and put on new clothes. I felt a little bit better but was still dizzy. I ventured into the front room and dropped myself onto the couch like a bag of potatoes.

Massaging my shoulder, I tried to remember what exactly happened last night. I was looking at that photo of the Southern soldier and then I was swept into the photograph, into the Civil War. It was all coming back to me; the Southern solider, his death, the rifle shot pushing its way into the back of my shoulder, the escape from the union soldiers, the doctor, the extraction of the bullet; and finally, the red-hot knife that cauterized my wound causing me to pass out.

As I was resting, my shoulder would get sharp, stabbing pains. I decided to go and take a couple pain pills, so slowly I got my body to stand up and start moving. I was heading down the hallway when the front doorbell rang. I stopped and went to see who would be coming to see me on my day of rest. I opened the door and there she was.

"Rebecca?" I said in a surprised voice.

"Hi stranger." She said with her low sexy voice, standing there as beautiful as ever. "Long time no see. How have you been? I hope I'm not disturbing you."

"Of course not, would you like to come in?" I asked as I opened wide the door and carefully (the pain was still there) extended my arm and hand into the direction of my front room. We both walked into the front room, Rebecca sitting in the chair and I on the couch.

"So how have you been?" she asked with her dark blue eyes meeting mine.

"I've been fine. I've missed you."

"It has been a while. I'm sorry I haven't stopped by sooner."

"No, no. I am the one that should be sorry for not trying to get ahold of you."

"What have you been doing lately?"

"Working on the family tree and watching my grandson, Peter, participate in a Civil War reenactment at the park."

"That sounds like fun."

"I went and saw the reenactment last Saturday. It was great with all the uniforms and rifles. The cannons and all the smo..."

"David" ... Her voice cut into my conversation. She got up from the chair and came to sit next to me on the couch. "Why haven't you called or stopped by to see me?" She sat there gazing into my eyes. Her perfume, White Diamonds, I breathed in, and I was wondering myself why I had not tried to seek her out. I reached out and put her hands in mine.

"Rebecca, I have missed you so much." I said sincerely. "I just wanted to give you some space, but I would really like to see more of you."

"I would like that too." She said with her Mona Lisa smile.

"Dinner tonight?"

"Sounds good." She answered.

Suddenly there was a spasm pain in my shoulder. I grabbed my shoulder and winced. Rebecca touched my arm and looked at me with great concern.

"What's wrong? Are you hurt?" She asked as I am sure my face showed a torturous expression.

"I think I just slept on my shoulder wrong. I'll make an appointment with the doctor today and have it checked out." I went to stand up but the pain in my shoulder pulled me back down and I found myself once again sitting face to face with Rebecca.

"You need to go to see your doctor or even check into the hospital." Rebecca said as she stared into my face.

"You are right. Can you call for me? The doctor's number is in the kitchen on the side of the refrigerator." Rebecca stood up, picked the phone off the corner of the couch and went into the kitchen. I could hear her talking to Dr. Jack Stanley. She indicated that I was experiencing some great discomfort in my shoulder, and she felt I needed to come into the doctor's office today. I heard her say "Goodbye" and then she walked back into the front room and placed the phone back into its holder.

"Dr. Stanley will see you in an hour. So, we better get ready to go." How can one be so forceful with such a loving sounding voice? She was like an angel from heaven with a whip making sure the task was done. She helped me stand and with her assistance I got my coat on. "I'll drive." She said as we headed out the door. I wasn't going to argue!

Since she was not sure how to get to Dr. Stanley's office, I was the navigator for our trip. It only took 15 minutes to arrive, so we sat in the car for a while.

"I want to thank you for doing this. It really wasn't necessary. I could have driven over here."

"With your shoulder being in that much pain, I don't think that would be a wise decision." Rebecca said. "Sounds like you did more than just sleep on it wrong. Did you accidently hit your shoulder?"

"Tell you what. I will tell you all at lunch after meeting with the good doctor. Deal?"

"Deal. Now let's get you in to see the good doctor." She opened her driver's side door and exited. I managed to get out of the car, but the pain was still with me. I was glad she had come. I really don't think it would have been a wise decision to drive and all this has given me time to talk with Rebecca. I really have been missing her. I wanted to restart our relationship again and see where it could go.

We walked into the doctor's office. I signed in, waved at the receptionist, and took a seat next to Rebecca.

"Dr. Stanley is a great doctor." I start the conversation. "He and I play golf when he has the time. I think, sometimes, he doesn't want to play golf with me because I'm usually play better than him."

"I'm sure with your shoulder feeling the way it does today, he would be very happy to play some golf with you!" She said with a little turned up smile on her face and those eyes looking into mine.

"I'm sure he would. Please don't suggest that today!" I responded to her. She smiled and returned her gaze to the magazine she was reading. The door had opened, "Mr. Harlow." The nurse was ready for me to follow her into the examination room. Rebecca stayed behind and waved as the door closed behind me. Once in the examine room, I took a seat on the examine table. About five minutes later the door opened and in stepped Dr. Jack Stanley.

"Well, well, well, if it isn't my old golf buddy. How are you doing these days?" That was Dr. Jack's approach, quick and to the point.

"I seem to have an issue with my shoulder. I am experiencing some sharp pin-like pain."

"Let's get the shirt off and we can take a look." I removed my shirt, and he started the examination.  He was looking at the front of my body. "Right or left side?" He asked.

"Right side." I moved my hand over the spot where the pain was.

"Let's see." He said as I lowered my hand, and he placed his hand on the right front shoulder area. He moved his over the area and finally hit the right spot.

"That's it, right there." I said as a tear formed in the corner of my eye where the spot was examined. As the doctor was feeling the front on my shoulder, his other hand started feeling the spot on the back side of my body. He suddenly jumped a little as his hand that had been examining my back side moved quickly off my body. He walked around to the back of my body, on the right side, and saw a six-inch scar on my shoulder. It looked like some kind of branding on the back of my shoulder. It was a contracture scar, flat and shiny. It was healed looking like it must be at least a year or more in age.

"Dave. What the hell did you do, or someone do to your back shoulder?" The doctor was in complete shock. He closely looked at the scar, feeling all around it. He then went to the medical folder on Dave. Dave's last examine was six months prior but no record of the scar. "I could get an x-ray of this, but it won't tell me anything." He said as came around to the front of me, looking at me and again asking. "Dave, what happen?"

"I hesitate to say anything because you may not believe me."

"Try me." Jack said with a puzzled expression on his face. "I am all ears." He walked over to a chair in front of the exam table where I was sitting and sat down. "You have my undivided attention." I vacillated, looking around the room, then at Jack.

"OK. The scar is from a Civil War bullet I received yesterday; well sort of yesterday." I was looking straight at Jack being as honest as possible. Jack looked at me and smiled.

"Try again, Dave. That scar is at least a year old if not older. Did you get it when you were around one of those Civil War reenactments? I hear they hold those in a park nearby."

"Yes, they did hold reenactments in the park. My grandson was a Southern soldier in the last one held last Saturday; and no, I did not get shot at a reenactment."

"Ok, can I give up, where and when?" I hesitated again as I tried to find my next words. Finally, they came out fast and furious.

"I got shot by a Northern soldier on May 18th, 1864. I ran after I got shot and found my way to a Southern encampment where the doctor proceeded to remove the bullet and then because he could not stop the bleeding, the doctor heated up his knife and cauterized my wound. And that is how I got the scar." There was silence in the room. Jack and I were looking at each other, but no one was speaking.

"I am afraid to ask but how did you end up in 1864, Dave?" Jack asked with disbelief in his eyes.

"I was looking at a photograph of a Southern soldier and somehow, I don't understand how, but I was pulled into that photograph, and I found myself standing behind the photographer taking the picture of that same soldier. Jack, I know you don't believe me, but it's the truth."

"This is the same story you told me six months ago. I didn't believe you then and I don't believe you now. However, with that being said, it would explain how you've got a scar that is more than a year old, in an area where six months ago there was no scar. Also, what is intriguing is if you look closely at the scar, there are a couple areas where it looks like the end point of a knife." Jack took a deep breath after making his statement.

"So, let's say it is true, which it is, how long would you think this pain will exist in my shoulder?"

"I have no idea. If you had that happen to you today, I would say that it would take about six months plus before you would stop noticing the pain. In your case it really didn't happen yesterday, but it did happen yesterday. Look at me; I am not making any sense. Hell, this whole thing doesn't make sense!" Jack had started shaking his head. He got up from his chair and started wandering around the room and talking to himself. He stopped at looked at me, "Dave, I have no idea how long it will take to heal. What am I saying, the scar has already healed. So, maybe in six months plus, the pain will dissipate. There, that is my medical opinion."

"I can tell you don't believe me, and you didn't believe me six months ago when I talked to you about being pulled into the photograph of my relatives and spending time face to face with them. I don't blame you. I don't think I would believe it if roles were reversed. However, what I told you did happen, and the scar is my proof."

"Well, I must say, the scar is a very convincing argument, but time travel is impossible; that is a scientific fact!"

"I have no argument on that. There is no scientific fact, but it happened to me. How, I don't know how, but it did." I was now speaking in a very low tranquil voice trying to calm Jack down. "Jack, do me a favor. Take a picture with your phone and send it to me. I need to see the scar myself." Jack took his phone out from the pocket in his doctor's coat and positioned the phone directly over my scar.

"Smile." Jack said, breaking the silence that was in the room. "There, I just sent it to your phone." Jack backed up a little and then looking at me said, "Dave, I know you are not crazy, at least not to the extreme!" I know Jack was trying to lighten the mood. "I just have a hard time believing all this. Do you have any proof, except for the scar, which I will admit is pretty good evidence, but any other item or proof that this was all real?" I thought about whether there would be any other proof that I could provide. Wait a minute, maybe there is.

"I might be able to get the proof you're wanting. When I was pulled into the photograph, I spent so much time talking to this Southern soldier. His name was Jimmy Bob Lansford of Charlton, Georgia. He had a wife named Samantha and a little girl named Abigail. While we were talking, he mentioned that he had written a letter to his wife and had made a necklace with a heart shaped locket for his daughter. He placed both in a tin container and buried it at the root of the tree we were sitting at. He then etched out a heart in the tree, so he could find it later. Jack, if I could find the tin with the letter and locket inside, would that be proof enough for you that I was there during at that period of time?"

"It would still be hard to believe all of this, but it certainly would get me closer to believing you were there. So, what is your plan?" I started to put my shirt back on.

"I'm going to the battlefield of Adairsville, which is just Northeast of Rome Georgia. I'm going to look for the tree with the heart etched on it and dig at the base of the tree. I'm going to find the tin."

"Dave, I hate to lie waste to your adventure, but that was one hundred and fifty years plus. Do you think that tree is still there? It's probably been torn down and a strip mall at that location or it's been paved over with cars driving on top of that tin. You must face reality. Wait a minute. Look who I am talking to; reality, that's an unknown word in your vocabulary."

"Jack, I know the site might not be there, but I must try. If it is still there, I can take a picture of the items proving that I was really there. I'll then send you the pictures. And if it's not there; well, I guess you can say I had a nice vacation…. into reality." We both smiled at each other. Jack took my hand and shook it.

"Good luck, my friend. I wish you good hunting." Jack opened the exam door, and I made my way into the reception area. Rebecca stood up as I entered the reception area.

"I see you're still alive." She said with a smile on her face. She linked her arm into mine. "How about I take you out to lunch?" she asked as we exited the doctor's office.

"No, lunch will be my treat. Remember I still need to pay for your taxi service!" I said with a smile on my face. This was nice, walking arm in arm with Rebecca.

## VI

We arrived at Rebecca's favorite restaurant downtown. After finding a place to park, we made our way to the eatery.

"Two?" the hostess asked as we walked inside.

"That will be fine." I said. We were shown to a booth next to a glass window where we could see the activities of the busy downtown area. We scanned our menu, and both ordered a chicken Caesar salad.

"So, what did the doctor say about your shoulder pain?" Rebecca asked as we waited for our food.

"There is a scar on my back shoulder which is the source of the pain. The scar has healed but you can still tell its location. This type of scar would normally take a year or more to get looking like it currently does. The thing the doctor was asking was why it was not there six months ago when I went in for my normal exam." I started the conversation, knowing where it would eventually end up at.

"So how did you answer him?"

"I need to tell you something and I am not sure how to say it."

"Dave, just tell me the truth. That's all it takes." After hearing that, I drank down some water and took a couple deep breaths.

"The truth? OK, the Truth." I took a couple more deep breaths. "Remember when we first met in the store parking lot and I had mistakenly called you by your grandmother's name, Alice."

"I slightly remember that."

"And then later you found a photograph of your grandmother and there was a man standing next to her that looked like me."

"Yes, I remember that, go on." I took more deep breaths.

"The truth is that man was me."

"What are you trying to say? That photograph was taken over a hundred years ago. How could that man be you?"

"About six months ago, I discovered that if I concentrated on a photograph, every detail of the photo's objects; the face, the eyes, the mouth, and the surrounding environment, I would be, and I don't know how, pulled into the photograph and experience being there, in that time period. I started to see the things and people that were in the photograph. Are you with me so far?" I looked across the table at Rebecca's blank look. Was she thinking, *how can I get away from this nut* or *am I in a dream and I am just pretending he has just said that.* "There's more. Do you want me to go on?"

"Please do. This is fascinating." Somehow her look did not reflect that she was fascinated by what I was saying, but I went on.

"I had a photograph of New York City taken about 1900. I started studying the image, the dresses, the hats, the faces, the building and before I knew it, I was in New York City in about 1900, standing behind the photographer taking the picture. I walked around the city and experienced the sights and sounds, including the smell, of New York in 1900. I did meet your grandmother and we had lunch and then dinner and went to a show that night. That is where that photograph you found was taken, this adventure only lasted one day. Once I fall asleep, I'd wake up the next day back at my house."

The salads came and Rebecca asked for a bottle of their best white wine. We started eating, I didn't say anything, and I could not read her face, what she was thinking. The wine came and the waiter poured the wine into her glass, a full glass. After she had consumed most of her wine filled glass, she looked at me.

"Do you really want me to believe all of this? And what does that have to do with the scar on your back shoulder?"

"I wanted to tell you about how I met your grandmother through that photograph of New York City. Especially since you had that picture of your grandmother and me at the theater; you might believe that I could be absorbed into a photo image and experience that period of time." I took the bottle of wine and poured myself a small amount of wine. I drank the wine and then continued.

"The scar..." I paused for a few seconds more before continuing. "I was looking at a photo of a Southern soldier taken in 1864. And like times before, before I knew it, I was standing behind the photographer who was taking the picture. I spent time talking to the soldier and learnt his name, where he was from, his family and some of his thoughts of the war. I was sitting down at the base of a tree and he, his name was Jimmy Bob Lansford of Charlton, Georgia, stood up, facing me. He was shot and fell on top of me. I was able to push his body off of me and I started to run. I had run about a thousand feet when a bullet hit me in the shoulder. I fell down a ravine. I kept perfectly still until it started to get dark. I don't know how, but I was able to find my way, in that coming darkness, to a Southern encampment. There a doctor removed the bullet and then cauterized the spot to stop the bleeding, I passed out after that. The next thing I know is that I woke up in my house, on the floor." I took the bottle of wine and poured myself another small glass. I drank the wine and then looked up at Rebecca. She just seemed to sit there not knowing what to say. Finally, after what seemed an eternity, she spoke.

"So..." She started slowly, looking at me the whole time. "...do you have any proof of these adventures?

"I left little messages in the newspaper, which proved to me that it really occurred. The photograph of your grandmother, which I had forgotten about until you brought it to the restaurant that night. And now I have a scar from my last adventure which Dr. Jack Stanley could not explain how six months earlier I did not have a scar and now I have one that looks to be a year plus healed scar. I know this is hard to understand and believe and thank you for not getting up from the table, pointing your finger at me and yelling 'Madman, madman', and then running out of this restaurant".

"It was tempting, but you do seem to have some proof." Rebecca said while looking down at her plate and playing with the last of her salad. She stopped playing with her salad and looked at me. "Are you the only one that has experienced this?"

"I've never heard of anyone else. When this first started, six or so months ago, I thought I was going crazy. That is why I started leaving myself little messages in the newspaper just to convince myself. When I woke up the next day, I would search the newspapers of that time and found the messages. I am now going to take on new research to try and prove all this really did happen."

"What are you going to do?" She asked with great interest.

"In this last adventure, while I was talking to Jimmy Bob Lansford, he had placed a letter and necklace with a locket in a tin and buried at the base of a tree. He then marked the tree with a heart and the initials of JL +SL. I am going to go to that battlefield and try to locate that tin. It will be the proof I need to show Dr. Jack and you that I am not crazy."

"Dave, I don't think you are crazy. A great imagination maybe but like you said you do have some proof all ready. Can I go with you?"

"Can you go with me? That would be fantastic! When can you leave?"

"I can leave anytime."

"Great. I will make all the reservations and we can leave in a couple days."

"You do realize that that tree may be grown over and may not even exist anymore."

"Yes, I have thought about it, but I must give it a try. I've got nothing to lose and everything to gain! Are you done here; I want to get started."

"Yes, sure." She said as she wiped her face with her napkin and rose from the table.  Dave followed suit, leaving money on the table, and kept in step behind Rebecca out of the restaurant. They arrived shortly at Dave's house. Both had exited the car and made their way into the house. Once inside, Rebecca asked to see Dave's scar on the back of his shoulder. He removed his shirt and turned his back towards Rebecca. She slowly placed her hand on the scar, feeling the bumps and ridge, agreeing with Dr. Jack Stanley's assessment that the scar definitely looked to be a year old or older.  If Dr. Stanley had not seen this scar, which is hard to miss, six months ago, then something unexplained did occur and backs up Dave's account even more.

"Seen enough?" Dave asked and with Rebecca nodding her head, he proceeded to put his shirt back on. Rebecca took out her phone, sat on the couch, and started working on a search. Dave, having redressed, sat next to Rebecca, and watched her as she worked on her phone. She was searching for the names of the Southern soldier that had died in the month of May 1864.

*Jimmy Bob Lansford of Charlton, Georgia, died May 17, 1864.*

His name was the 26th name listed. Rebecca had never realized that there was a Charlton, Georgia. She had always known about a Charleston, South Carolina, but not a Charlton in Georgia. She turned her head towards Dave.

"You are right. There was a Jimmy Bob Lansford of Charlton, Georgia that died on May 17, 1864." Her eyes got big as she looked at this man whose wild story just might be true! She stood up immediately, "I am going home to pack. Call me when you are ready to go, I'll be ready!" She headed for the front door, only to turn facing Dave and said, "Dave, I love you!"

The door closed quietly behind her while Dave stared toward that door thinking about the words he had just heard.

"I better start making some reservations!"

# VII

The plane departed the airport on time with Dave and Rebecca relaxed in their seats with a couple of glasses of white wine.

"I am so glad you decided to go with me on this exploration." Dave started the conversation. Nothing much had been said up to this point regarding his confession of the adventures he had encountered, but now twenty thousand feet in the air and with a couple glasses of wine before them, this looked like the perfect time to discuss it. "So do you believe me when I told you about my adventures?"

"It's really hard to believe the stories..." She started out. "...but some of the things I saw and heard were hard not to discount."

"Like what?" I pushed her.

"The fact that I saw the death listing of your Southern solider you were talking about and that scar that your doctor said was not there six months ago; and that photograph I found of you and my grandmother. It's really hard not to believe with these facts and I don't believe you are crazy or are going through a mental breakdown. There's also the fact that I think I am falling in love with you, so you can't be crazy, please." She looked so seriously into my eyes and all I could do was display a big smile and I reached over and put her hands into mine.

"I promise you; I am not insane. Occasionally crazy, here and there."

"Oh, stop it." Rebecca said with that beautiful smile returning to her face.

"The only thing I'm crazy about is you."

"Oh Dave, I'm crazy about you too."

"So, see, we are both a little crazy!" We both laughed and then she reached over and kissed Dave. He knew then the rest of this trip was going to be fine.

The plane arrived at the Atlanta airport right on time, 10:38 am. Dave had rented a car and he and Rebecca were soon on the road to Adairsville, Georgia. It took a little over an hour to reach the city of Adairsville with a population a little over forty-six hundred. After checking into the local hotel, the couple headed towards the small visitor's center in the middle of town.

"We are looking for the Civil War battlefield that took place here or bouts on May 17th, 1864. Can you help us?" Dave was speaking to the elderly woman seated behind the counter of the visitor's center. The woman stood up and centered a map of Adairsville and its surrounding areas in front of Dave and Rebecca.

"Well, in May of 1864, there was a lot of fighting happening close to the Robert C. Saxon House, otherwise known as the Gravel House." She was pointing to an area just north of the town. "Eight Tennessee Regiments posted here, defended it during several hours of musketry and artillery fire, finally withdrawing at midnight."

"How far is this Gravel House?" Rebecca was asking.

"Oh, it's about two to two and a half miles north on US 41."

"Are there many trees around the area?" Dave asked.

"Well, there still might be a few. There is a historical landmark stating where the battle was. You can't miss it. There is not too much of anything else out there. After the Civil War, this whole area was rebuilt and became a center of the carpet and textile industries. After that it all kind of faded away. Then in 2013 we were hit by an EF3 tornado and flatten mostly everything. The town is slowly being rebuilt, but it takes a while. You folks from out of town?"

"We are. We're just interested in some of the Civil War battlefields." Dave explained.

"Well, like I said, not too much to see, but it's out there." The woman had a very warm smile that was contagious. Dave and Rebecca smiled back at her and then thanked her for all her insight. The couple exited the visitor center and returned to their car.

"It's getting kind of late. How about dinner, and then tomorrow morning, we hit the battlefield?" Dave said he could tell Rebecca was getting tired and it had been a long day.

"Sounds like a plan." Rebecca responded.

Dave drove around downtown, but most of the small restaurants were closed or closing, so they wandered out to US 41 and found several open eateries. Dave asked Rebecca to choose one and they settled on a Chinese restaurant close to their hotel.

Morning came early the next day and after grabbing breakfast at the hotel, they headed out on US 41 for about 2 miles. We saw a stone plaque standing on the side of the road, so we pulled over to investigate. We both got out of the car and walked over to the plaque. It talked about Adairsville, Georgia:

> *Adairsville had its beginning in Oothcaloga Valley, two miles north of the present site. It was named for Cherokee Indian Chief John Adair, the son of a Scottish trader and a Cherokee Princess.*
> *Adairsville moved in 1848 to Adair Station (established 1846 by William Watts) but kept the name Adairsville, honoring the Indian Chief.*
> *The Battle of Adairsville, sometimes known as the "Gravel House Battle" was fought May 17, 1864.*

*Adairsville was entered in the National Register of Historic Places Dec. 4, 1987. The nomination was prepared by the Sans Souci Club's Historical Committee: Lois S. Adams, Chairman, Carol T. Adams, Ovalle P. Barton, Odella R. Hayes, Martha K. Johnson, & Pansy O. Penfield.*

*Chief John Adair - Born 1790's*
*Adairsville Incorporated in 1854*
*Great Locomotive Chase - April 12, 1862*

"So, this is the area you talked about." Rebecca said as she finished reading the dedication.

"This is it." Dave said as he looked around. Nothing looked familiar. There weren't too many trees around the area, only that small cluster about a half a mile down the road. "Let's head down the road a bit, towards those trees." Dave was pointing down the road. They both got back into the car and headed down to their destination. They arrived at the cluster of trees and exited the vehicle. Dave looked around trying to remember that day talking to Jimmy and taking in his surroundings. "This could be it. I just don't know. I can't remember any of this. Let's spread out.  Look at the base of the trees; we are looking for a heart shaped etching with the initials JL + SL."

"Alright." Rebecca said as she started investigating the trees opposite of Dave. They both examined the entire tree, top and bottom, as they moved from one wood timber to another. It must have been about twenty minutes when Rebecca stopped in her tracks. There before her, about eye level, was a faint etching of a heart. She touched it with her hand and moved it over the faded initials, JI.SI. "Dave, come over here." She shouted in Dave's direction. Dave heard her calling and dashed over to her location. He stood there in awe next to Rebecca. She was still rubbing her hand over the etching. "It looks like the bottom part of the letter 'L' has faded, leaving the letter 'I' and the '+' is completely disappeared."

"This must be the tree. The carving has moved up with the growth of the tree these hundred plus years. The heart he carved out is almost gone but you can still faintly see it." Dave now had his hand moving over the etching along with Rebecca's. "If this is the tree…" Dave's eyes moved down to the base of the tree.

"Find something to dig with!" Rebecca said excitedly. Dave looked around but could not find a substitute shovel.

"Wait a minute…" Dave said as he rushed back to the rental car. He returned with a tire iron that came with the car to remove the bolts from the tires when you might need to change them. Dave dropped to his knees and using the small but flat edge of the tire iron, he proceeded to dig directly below the point where the faded heart's bottom point was. "Keep an eye out for any approaching vehicle or person. I don't want anyone to think I'm destroying this tree."

"Understood." Rebecca responded as she glanced at the 360 degrees around her and Dave's position. Dave continued to pierce the earth with all his strength. Five minutes of hole digging and surveillance, they heard the sound. The metal of Dave's digging tool and the existence of some kind of metal in the ground. Dave stopped and looked up to Rebecca. Her eyes were now on him with a look of surprise and anticipation. Could it be? Dave now used his hands to dig into the ground. Rebecca had dropped to her knees and was joining Dave on the quest for discovery. They slowly dug around the object, so not to damage it and being careful not to be cut by any metal edges. The digging went on for about ten minutes, but it was time well spent. Before them in the ground was a very old tin box. They carefully removed any remaining dirt from the side of the tin and then Dave put his hand under the object and slowly brought it into the sunlight. He lightly placed it on the ground between Rebecca and himself.

"This is it, Rebecca." Dave said, just staring at the tin box.

"So open it." Rebecca said excitedly. Dave carefully grabbed the top of the tin container and lifted it up. The top of the container separated from the body of the object exposing its contents. Dave and Rebecca's heads moved directly over the object, their cheeks touching each other. They both had a clear view of the contents of the tin. It was a paper, folded several times. Dave removed the letter; below the removed letter was a necklace at the bottom of the tin. Dave slowly opened the letter, which he discovered was actually several pages, while Rebecca carefully removed the necklace from the tin. Dave started to read the letter out loud.

May 17, 1864

My precious wife, Samantha, the love of my life. I sit here under the shade of this tree with the smell and worries of this war all around me, but all I can think about is you. I did not have to leave when I did, but I had to go fight with my brothers, I hope you understand. I wish I could turn back the hands of time and just say "Go without me!", but I couldn't. I miss your touch and your body lying next to mine. I can always see your blue eyes and your flowing golden hair in my dreams. Your lips, so moist and longing. The soft gentle way you would talk to me as we would dream about our future. I know when this war is over, we can pick up that dream and move forward.

The war just seems to go on and on. My brothers in arm long for the day it will end. There is so little food and supplies. Our blankets and shoes are all worn so thin. Even tobacco is running in short supply. I hope the war doesn't last another year, I do not think we could last another winter.

Please give kisses and hugs to my little Abigail. Tell her daddy misses bouncing her on my knee and giving her bear hugs and kisses. She must be getting big by now. I can't believe it's been three years since I left.

I love you both so much. God bless you and keep you safe until I can put my loving arms around you both.

Love Jimmy

Dave and Rebecca just sat there on the ground, tears streaming down their faces.

"That was beautiful, Dave. I'm glad you were there for him." Dave looked up from the letter and into Rebecca's eyes.

"So, you believe me when I said I was here."

"Yes, how else could you have known about the tin? I don't know how it happened, but I do believe it did." Dave's face lit up with a big giant smile. Then he turned his attention to the hole they had created.

"Let's push the dirt back into the hole." Dave said as he, and Rebecca, used their hands and slowly filled the hole back to its original appearance. Afterwards Dave and Rebecca sat on the ground with their backs to the bark of the tree. They both looked at their dirty hands and clothes.

"Now what?" Rebecca asked as they sat there.

"Well, first thing first. I am going to lay out the tin, the letter, and the necklace. Take my phone and snap a few pictures of the items along with a picture of the tree and the faded heart and initials. Later I will send the pictures to Dr. Jack Stanley to maybe help him believe in my story." Dave took his pictures, gathered up the tin, the letter, and the necklace. "I think we should go back to the hotel and clean up a bit and then we make our way to the library to do some more research."

"What kind of research?" she asked inquisitively.

"Jimmy Bob Lansford of Charlton, Georgia. I want to see if his relatives may still be living in Charlton. I understand that the Adairsville Library may not have the information, then that means we'll be off to Charlton, Georgia." Dave stood up and extended his hand to Rebecca to help her stand. They made their way to the car and then drove back to the hotel.

# VIII

It took just under six hours to drive from Adairsville, Georgia to Charlton County, Georgia with a population of just under thirteen thousand. The roads were fairly clear, and the scenery was well worth the drive. They found the Charlton County library in the little town of Folkston, with a population of twenty-five hundred. Before doing their investigation, Dave decided to find some lodging. A bed and breakfast was found for them, and the lodging recommended a nice local restaurant where they could enjoy some fine Folkston food. The decision was to rest and fill up today and hit the library tomorrow after breakfast.

The next morning, they found the county library. It was a small library, way smaller than what they were used to. The library did have a research section and the two of them started researching.

Jimmy Bob Lansford had married Samantha Harper in January of 1860. The Lansford's had a girl born to them in November of 1860 named Abigail.

Abigail married John Berry, ten years her senior, in 1878 and lived on the Lansford farm. Abigail and John Berry had nine children, three boys and six girls, three of the girls died in infancy. The eldest son, John Jr., stayed on the farm while the other children married and moved to surrounding cities.

John Jr. married Mildred Johnstone in February of 1909. Their union produced five girls; all would live to adulthood and married.

The eldest daughter, Bertha Bell, married Thomas Gilmore in 1930 and had three boys and two girls. Bertha and Thomas remained on the farm, enlarged its acreage, and produced twice the crop it had in the past. They renamed the Lansford Farm to Gilmore Ranch in 1945.

Bertha and Thomas' eldest son, Ronald, married Gail Gladstone in May of 1960. Their union produced two sons and one daughter. Gail passed away at the turn of the century and Ronald, now 81, has since retired but is still living on the ranch. His eldest son, Philip and his wife, Jacqueline, run the operation of the ranch.

Gilmore Ranch is about one hundred and ten acres with a large two-story home; five bedrooms, dining room, family room, and large kitchen built in the center of the ranch. It's located two miles north of the Charlton County line.

Dave and Rebecca left the library with directions on how to arrive at the Gilmore Ranch. They drove the two miles north of the Charlton County line and arrived at the ranch just after noontime. Turning on to the entrance of the ranch and going under the sign above them that said Gilmore Ranch; the two were just taking in the size of this property. They drove up to the large two-story house painted in earth tones, and accented in bright red. After they stopped, they just looked at each other.

"Imagine. I am sure that when Jimmy Bob lived here it was probably only a tenth of the size." Dave said as the two of them exited the car.

"What are you going to say?" Rebecca asked as they made their way to the front door.

"I am going to play it by ear!" Dave said as he pressed the doorbell. Before long the door opened. There in the doorway was a beautiful, five-foot nine woman, dressed in jeans, boots, and a western style shirt; her hair was made up in a bun.

"Yes, can I help you?" The lady of the house asked.

"Hello, my name is Dave Harlow, and this is my friend, Rebecca Langford. We have some information regarding the family tree of Philip Gilmore that we would like to share. Is Philip home?"

"Why yes he is, please come in."

Dave and Rebecca were shown into a large library where a man, six foot three, was revealed to them to be Philip Gilmore. Everyone exchanged introductions and then sat in the room's couch and chairs. Dave, sitting on the couch next to Rebecca, started the conversation.

"I have come into possession of a letter that was written by Jimmy Bob Lansford to Samantha Lansford back in 1864 and I would like to pass it onto someone in the family line." Dave slowly, and carefully, removed the tin and then the letter within the tin from his jacket, opened the letter and placed it on the table in front of Philip. Philip sat up on his chair and began reading the letter.

Dave removed the necklace from the tin. "Here is a necklace…" Dave placed in front of Philip. "… that Jimmy Bob made for his daughter, Abigail. Both the letter and the necklace never reached Samantha or Abigail." Philip and Jacqueline both read the letter and looked at the necklace.

"And how much do you want for these items?" Philip asked as he glared at Dave and Rebecca.

"Philip, you misunderstood. We don't want anything for the items. I am currently working on my own family tree line, and I thought you would like to have these items."

"I apologize. I do follow my family tree, and these are indeed unique items. Jimmy Bob Lansford was the start of my family tree, even though I don't even know what my Great-Great-Great Grandfather or Great-Great Grandmother looked like."

"I can't help you with your great-great grandmother Abigail, but here…" Dave pulled out the picture of Jimmy Bob Lansford he had on his desk and had brought it with him, just in case. "…is a photograph of Jimmy Bob Lansford."

"How did you come into the possession of these items?" Philip asked.

"Antique stores and a lot of research. I was fascinated by the items and wanted to find a family member who would appreciate them. I am hoping you are that person."

"I definitely am. Ever since I discovered that my grandfather had renamed this property from Lansford Farm to Gilmore Ranch, I wanted to know more about the Lansford line. I was able to trace the Lansford name to Jimmy Bob; and I know he was killed in the Civil War; but could not find out anything prior to Jimmy Bob."

"The only other thing I discovered was that Jimmy Bob was born on the Lansford Farm and took it over when his parents died." Dave stood up and signaled Rebecca to do the same. Philip and Jacqueline also stood. "I feel that my purpose has been fulfilled. I thank you both for your time and for allowing me to share a little bit of your history. It has been an adventure. Before we leave, would you mind if I took a picture of the two of you?"

"Of course not." Philip said as he posed with his wife in front of the fireplace. Dave took out his phone and snapped a couple of pictures.

After the photo session, the four of them moved to the front door, as Philip and Jaqueline again said 'Thanks' for the items and let them know the objects would be placed with the other family tree treasures. The door closed and Dave and Rebecca looked at each other with big smiles.

They walked to the rental car and after getting inside, Dave took out his phone and sent the pictures of the tin, the letter, the necklace, the tree that held these treasures, along with the picture of the faded heart and initials of Jimmy Bob Lansford and his wife, Samantha Lansford to Dr. Jack Stanley. This was the proof he had promised Jack when he was in Jack's office. In addition, Dave included the photograph of Philip and Jacqueline Gilmore along with the message: The trip was a success!

*Attached are pictures of the tin which contained the letter that Jimmy Bob Lansford wrote and the necklace he made for his daughter, Abigail. Finally, I have included a picture of Philip and Jacqueline Gilmore, the great-great-great grandfather of Jimmy Bob Lansford. You asked for more proof of my adventure and here it is. I hope this will help prove that the impossible was made possible.*

# IX

Dr Jack Stanley was standing at the door outside his next patient when his phone made a noise indicating that a text message had come through. He stopped, reached for his phone, and read the text from Dave Harlow. He reviewed the pictures and Dave's final words: "…*proof that the impossible was made possible.*" Jack had requested proof that Dave had somehow slipped into a photograph he was looking at. Dave had met that request. Jack was now looking at the pictures and remembering the scar he had seen on Dave's back shoulder. That scar that was not there six months prior. Jack found a chair outside the patient's door and sat down, shaking his head all the way down. He knew that logic told him that Dave could not look at a photograph and then be somehow sucked into the picture, but the scar and the pictures were telling a different story. Jack started to reply to Dave's text and pictures, his fingers moving across the keyboard, his head shaking in disbelief the whole time. He hit the send button, stood up and moved into his next patient's room.

A few thousand miles away, Dave's phone vibrated indicating he had an incoming text message. He looked at his phone and smiled. It simply said, "I Believe!"

The flight home was most enjoyable for Dave and Rebecca. They talked about the digging at the base of the tree, finding the letter and necklace of Jimmy Bob Lansford. They shared their excitement of meeting the relatives of Jimmy Bob and Samantha. Dave was glad he took a picture of the letter and necklace before turning the treasures over to Phillip and Jacqueline Gilmore. Dave shared the text message he received from Jack with Rebecca. This was exciting. They also shared their feelings with each other, with Dave acknowledging that he wanted to take their love for each other more seriously.

"Now that we have experienced this adventure together, do you believe what I told you about being pulled into photographs and participating in that day's event?" Dave asked as he looked into Rebecca's blue eyes.

"It's still hard to believe that it really happened, however, when I saw with the etching Jimmy Bob had done on the tree, his hidden treasures, and the scar on your shoulder, I am almost….one hundred percent…. a believer."

"I can't turn down those odds! I have another story to tell you." Dave told Rebecca of being pulled into his honeymoon photo, spending time with his younger wife and a younger version of himself. He told her about the conversation with Helen and her comment about love being forever. That you can have enough love for your past and your future. "It was her way of telling me that I would not be dishonoring my love from the past and can love someone in the present…and that someone is you, Rebecca." Tears flowed down Rebecca's cheeks, and she kissed Dave on his cheek.

For the rest of the flight they talked about family. Rebecca remembered her eighth birthday in the late fifties with her mom and dad and all her friends. It was a great time that she could still see, though she was only eight. Dave opened up about his uncle, his mother's brother, George.

"I remember attending his thirtieth birthday party…" Dave started. "I was only seven and most of the people there were adults and a few cousins, but I did admire George. He was always so much fun; he acted like a kid himself. He would make up stories and joke around and make everyone around him laugh. And he drove the coolest car, a 1964 Plymouth Barracuda, with a slanted back. It was a cool looking car, at least to a seven-year-old."

"He sounds like a great guy. Is he still alive?"

"Unfortunately, not. He died that same night of his party."

"Oh my gosh, what happen?"

"After the party, he, his girlfriend, and another couple decided to walk to a local theater.  He was killed crossing the street by a hit and run driver. They never found the driver. The whole family was devastated when we heard the news and I guess that event stuck in my mind. That is why I remember that last party, that last time I saw him."

"How sad, Dave."

"I'm not sad. I am grateful I had the time, as little as it was, to know someone like that who could bring joy to people around him. And yes, he did make an impression on me and my life. I continue trying to bring joy and laughter to the people I meet."

"Well, that is why I love you. You bring joy and laughter into my life." We both looked into each other's eyes and then we kissed. The rest of the flight we talked about different members of each other's family. The loved ones and the not so warm ones; trying to find the best in the latter.

"Do me a favor when we get home." Dave asked Rebecca. "See if you can find a photograph of your eighth birthday party. I want to try something."

"Okay, but why?" she asked inquisitively.

"I want to try something, but I don't want to tell you just now. Trust me!"

"I will do my best. I'm sure I have some old photos in my closet."

"Thanks." Dave said with a smile on his face.

The plane landed and Dave drove Rebecca to her house, and she started looking for the requested photo. It took about an hour before she presented Dave with a black and white snapshot of an eight-year-old Rebecca standing among ten or twelve of her friends. Rebecca had long curly hair tied up in a ponytail. Her dress was long, stopping just below her knees. She had bobby socks and Mary Jane shoes to complete her outfit. The girls in the picture had similar clothing and the boys were dressed in jeans and plaid short-sleeve shirts. It looked like the group had just finished playing pin the tail on the donkey and were gearing up to sing Happy Birthday to the birthday girl with a large cake and lit candles sitting in front of the eight-year-old Rebecca.

"Is this what you were looking for? Rebecca asked Dave.

"This is perfect. I will return it back to you in a couple days if that is alright?"

"That will be fine." Rebecca answered. "What are you planning to do with it?"

"That is my secret. I will return it in a couple days, I promise." Dave said, smiling at her. "I am going to leave you for now; give you a chance to rest up after our flight. It will give me a chance to rest and clean up my house that I have been neglecting this past week. I will call you in a couple days and we can do dinner, okay?"

"That will be fine. I do need to get some rest after all that has happened this week. Call me."

"I will. I promise. I do love you."

"I love you too." She responded and gave him a heartfelt kiss on his lips.

Dave returned the kiss and then excused himself and left Rebecca's house grinning ear to ear. This is the happiest he has felt in a very long time. He felt like a kid of fifteen or sixteen. He turned up the radio loudly as he drove towards his house, singing along with the 60's tune, tapping on the steering wheel.

He reached his house in record breaking time, singing all the way up the walkway. Opening his front door, he placed his suitcase just inside the door, went to the couch and fell into the arms of the cushions. He fell asleep with a grin on his face and sweet dreams on their way.

Dave awoke two hours later, still having a big smile on his face. He made himself some coffee, picked up his suitcase and took it to his room. There he proceeded to empty its contents back into his dresser drawers. He found Rebecca's photograph she had given to him, and he stared at the photo. He was wondering if he could do the same thing with this snapshot as he had done with earlier photos. If he could do it again, what would he say to Rebecca's parents as far as who he was and what was he doing at the birthday party. Dave had to think this one out before proceeding.

It didn't take long before Dave had put together a plan in his mind and was ready to test his plan out. He rushed into the family tree room and picked up the magnifying glass and then, with the photograph in his hand, made his way to the comfortable chair in his bedroom. He put his feet up on the ottoman and started to examine the black and white photo. Dave looked at the details of Rebecca's dress and her friends' shoes. Then he stared deeper at the faces of the children, noting their smiles, their hair styles, their body positions. Slowly Dave could feel himself being pulled in. Slowly he could see their faces moving from side to side. Slowly he could…

# X

"Happy Birthday to you. Happy Birthday to you. Happy Birthday dear Rebecca. Happy birthday to you!"

I was standing behind an elderly gentleman with gray and white hair, balding on the back of his head taking the photograph. As I came around him, I could see the group of children, gathered around the table having just finished singing the Happy Birthday song to the girl standing in the middle of the group, looking down at the birthday cake. Before her was the cake with the eight candles illuminating her face. This girl with the long curly hair tied up in a ponytail was Rebecca.

"Excuse me." The elderly gentleman had turned his attention towards me. "Who the hell are you and what are you doing in my house!" I backed up a few inches raising both my hands in a surrender position.

"I am so sorry. My name is Dave Harlow, and I am with a local newspaper. Your door was wide open, I heard the children singing the Happy Birthday song and I just let myself in. I apologize for my entry into your house. My newspaper wanted me to follow up with some children's parties and report on how they may have differed throughout the years. Some of the activities have not changed for decades, whereas some new games may have been added to the party structure. Again, I do hope that my being here, observing the activities of the party, won't make this awkward for your family."

"No, I guess not. I just wished the newspaper would have called me up prior to the party to let me know they were sending someone."

"I totally agree with you. It was a short coming on actions of my office not to call you first. But since I am already here, is it alright that I stick around and watch? I promise not to be in the way at all." I tried to make this plead as sincere as possible. I stuck out my hand to the elderly gentleman hoping a shake of hands would secure my presents.

"I guess it will be okay." He said, completing the connection of the handshake. "My name is Frank, Frank Hanferd. Nice to meet you, Mr. Harlow."

"Just call me Dave."

"Okay, Dave. You can call me Frank."

"Thanks Frank. I'm just going to be like a fly on the wall, watching all the activities, taking notes, and staying out of the way." I explained to Frank as the party continued.

"Sounds good." Frank said as he hurried around the table, helping his wife to dish out the birthday cake sliced pieces, applying vanilla ice cream to each plate of birthday cake, and passing the plates to the children. The party continued with the opening of the birthday girl's presents, pin the tail on the donkey, and several board games. After about an hour, I walked over to Frank to make a suggestion.

"Frank…" He was just finishing up being a judge on a board game and turned his attention to my voice. "…may I make a suggestion of an activity I saw at another party?"

"Sure. Go ahead. I am open for suggestions." Frank was looking at me with an intuitive look.

"Why don't you have the children put together a time capsule. Get a coffee container or a metal box and have the kids fill the box. Then bury it in the ground in front of your house. I can do the digging if you like, and the boys and girls find items to put into the capsule."

"That is an interesting thought." Frank's brain was thinking about what he could use. "I have a metal box in the garage that I could use. I like the idea." He then turned his attention to the children in the room. "Boys and girls, we are going to create a time capsule, bury it and in the future dig it up to look at the items you placed in it. We will dig the hole; I need you boys and girls to find items to put into it."

The children yelled their positive acceptance to the idea and looked around the house, selecting the items to be buried. Frank handed me a shovel, then walked me outside, showing me the area where the hole was to be dug. In the meantime, Frank went into the garage to find the metal box that was to be used. I dug a two foot by two feet by three-feet-deep hole. Frank had gotten the metal box and was having the children place items in the box, I took the time to write a little note which I was going to place inside the time capsule. The metal box was filled almost to the top. I placed my note inside the box and the box was sealed; then placing it in the ground, I proceeded to cover the hole with the dirt I had just removed. Frank had made a little sign, *This time capsule was buried on Rebecca's Eighth birthday and should remain buried for a period of fifty years.*

"Fifty years! That's a long time. I will be dead when it's open." Frank was making this comment to me as I was standing by him.

"Yes, fifty years is a long time and yes most of us probably won't be around to dig it up; but for the people in the future who will be there, it will be a time of remembrance." I remarked back to Frank as the children finished this activity and hurried onto the next fun filled event. Frank quickly took the shovel I was holding and returned it back to the garage. I met Frank as he was exiting the garage and headed for the house.

"Frank, I am going to head out." I was shaking Frank's hand. I had caught him just before he headed back into the house. "I want to thank you for allowing me to watch all the activities you and your wife had planned out for this party. It turned out great. I think I have enough information for my news article. Thanks again."

"Sorry you have to leave. Thanks for digging that hole for the time capsule."

"Thanks for taking my suggestion for the time capsule. I think the children had fun finding items to place into the time capsule. Goodbye." I left the party and made my way to the boulevard close by where I found some food for my dinner.

After dinner, I made my way to a park close by. There I watched children go up and down the slides and swing on the swings. Soon the park was empty, and the moonlight was shining very brightly. I found an empty park bench and laid down. It wasn't long before I eyes close, and I fell sound to sleep.

# XI

The room was filled with daylight breaking through the curtains. I woke up in my chair staring at the ceiling. It took a few minutes before I could feel the blood return to my limbs and my head stop spinning. I rose up from my chair and slowly made my way to the kitchen where I made a fresh brew of coffee. I sat at the table and sipped my coffee. I was thinking about this latest adventure.

Rebecca's birthday would be tomorrow, and the time capsule would have reached its 50$^{th}$ anniversary. I picked up my phone and called Rebecca.

"Hello." She answered.

"Hi beautiful. Tomorrow is a very special day. How's about I pick you up around noontime, spend the day with you, and then take you out for dinner." I spoke with my most sincere voice.

"That sounds like a deal. I have some errands to run today but I will be dressed and ready to go tomorrow at noon."

"See you then…. I love you!" I said with my heart in my throat.

"I love you too. See you then." She confirmed.

"Bye."

"Bye."

The phone line went dead. Meeting her tomorrow would give me a chance to clean the house, which is sorely needed. I started in the kitchen and then moved on into the front room. I cleaned the bathroom and dusted my bedroom. Last, but not least, I straighten things in the family tree room. Organizing the photographs I had on the desk and filing them away. Among the snapshots, I came across the picture of my Uncle George's thirtieth birthday party. It was a black and white photograph. George, in the middle of the image; his friends and family surrounding him, holding up a glass, toasting him. I sat down in the chair and rested my arms on the desk, looking at the photo. Besides George, I could pick out my mother and father, my cousins and myself. The cousins and I ranged from six years old to twelve, me being seven. It was a great party. I remembered the fun I had playing with my cousins and listening to stories George would tell us during the day.

I picked up the magnifying glass and looked closer at everyone's expressions. Noting the clothes we were all wearing. Man has the clothing trends changed that much?! It's a good thing clothing designs have changed. I just kept looking at the shirt designs and the paisley designed dresses. I can't believe that people would go out in public like that. Look at the way the lines would crisscross and blend into…

# XII

The laughter was loud along with the music. I was again standing behind a man taking a photograph. That picture of George and the family. As I stepped around the photographer, I could see everyone that was in the photo including my seven-year-old self.

"One more time, cheers to George, Happy Birthday!" Someone yelled out.

"Cheers George and Happy Birthday." Multiple people responded, glasses were raised, and drinks consumed. I stayed in the background of the party just looking and listening to relatives that have been long gone. This was definitely a treat. After about an hour I made my way to George, the guest of honor.

"Happy birthday, George. This is a great party!" I said loudly to George, trying to be heard over the voices and music.

"Thank you." George responded with a questioned look on his face. "And who exactly are you? I'm sorry, I don't recognize you."

"I'm your 3rd cousin, Harry Osborne." I knew my aunt Osborne, who lived in New York and did have a son named Harry; neither would be here, so my deception would be safe. "I was visiting your city and heard about your birthday bash. I hope you don't mind that I showed up uninvited?"

"Not at all. Get yourself a drink and enjoy yourself. Glad to see you stopped by." George was sincere in his response, and I did feel welcome. I just needed to remember that I was Harry Osborne for the night.

The party went on for several hours. I did enjoy myself listening to George and his exaggerated stories about adventures he had taken (or made up in his mind). He definitely was the life of the party. About ten o'clock I saw him sneak out of the house. He had gone with his girlfriend, Mellissa, and another couple walking down the street towards downtown. I made my way out the door and headed to catch up with the group.

"So where is everybody going?" I asked, even though I already knew the answer.

"We are heading down to the local theater. They are having a special showing of Casablanca. That is one of my favorite movies and it's my birthday, so this birthday boy is going to treat himself. The others just wanted to tag along! And this beauty (he was holding Mellissa close, next to him) just wanted to be by my side." He leaned over and gave her a kiss on her cheek.

"Mine if I tag along. Casablanca is one of my favorites too." I said excitedly. Actually, I was not lying; Casablanca was in my top one hundred favorite films.

"Sure, come on. The more the merrier!" George said as we neared the street we would have to cross. The theater was just across the street. This was the street George would be killed by the hit and run driver. As we got closer to the street, my mind was thinking of what I could say to stop George from crossing the street.

"Hey, wait!" I shouted just as George's put his right foot onto the street to cross. Everyone stopped and looked in my direction. "Look over there." I pointed to the left and everyone's attention followed my hand. "The liquor store there at the corner. What if we bought our candy over there and then sneaked it into the theater.  It's a lot cheaper and they probably have a better selection." George's right foot came back onto the curb.

"Sounds like a great deal." George said with everyone shaking their heads. The group moved towards the liquor store talking about the last movie they had seen.

*I had done it! I prevented my uncle George from cross the street and getting killed by the hit and run driver!*

After making our candy selection and placing the loot inside our pockets, we left the liquor store and stopped at the street corner where there was a light. When we got the green walking man, we crossed the street safely, bought our tickets and made our way into the theater.

The hour and forty-two-minute movie ended, and we made our way out of the theater. We crossed the street with the light and walked past the liquor store we had visited earlier that evening. We walked what seemed to be a mile long (I did not remember it being this long when we walked to the movies earlier), but we were getting close. George was in front holding Mellissa's arm; I was directly behind them. The other couple was lagging behind about three hundred feet. We turned onto the next to the last street before his house and were halfway down the block, when we heard the screeching of wheels behind us.

A car racing on the streets had turned onto the street we were walking on. We all turned in the direction of the screeching car. It had turned the corner, but the driver had lost control of the car; zig zagging down the street heading towards George, Mellissa, and I. In a quick motion, George had pushed Mellissa into me, causing me and Mellissa to tumble onto the front lawn of a house. The car hit George directly, shooting him 100 feet into the air and landing in the driveway a couple houses down from Mellissa and myself. The car sped off, clipping off a rear-view mirror from a parked car along the street.

Mellissa and I hurried to George's side. The other couple was knocking on the door of a house closed by asking to use their phone because an accident had occurred and there were injuries. George was in bad shape. Mellissa held his one hand, and I held his other. George died before the ambulance could arrive.

The other couple helped a crying Mellissa back to George's house and explained to George's mother, my grandmother, and the other remaining guest what had happened (the younger me had already left the party earlier and went home). I stayed in the background listening to all the moans and tears that poured out from everyone. The police had arrived and spoke to my grandmother. She would need to come down to the hospital to officially identify George's body. As a family member took Grandma down to the hospital and the police finished their report, I made my way to the back yard and sat in a lawn chair staring up at the stars above me. Tears filled my eyes.

*I had changed the past. George did not die crossing the street. I stopped that. But I did not stop him from dying. I don't understand.*

I laid in the lawn chair weeping and after a couple hours I fell asleep.

# XIII

I woke up the next morning with my head on the desk in the family tree room. My eyes were wet with tears. I lifted my head up from the desk, but I was still deeply depressed. I sat in my chair for an hour before standing up and making my way to my bathroom. There I disrobed and got into the shower feeling the warm shower fall over my head and body. This adventure had been a hard one. To see my Uncle George once again and stopping his death by diverting everyone to a liquor store to purchase candies. I was flying high, then to be shot down so hard and so quickly by witnessing a different scenario of his death. I must have stayed in the shower for more than an hour, but it did do me some good. I got out of the shower, toweled myself off and went into my room, where I proceeded to dress myself for the day's task.

Today was Rebecca's birthday.

I arrived at Rebecca's house a little before noon. After knocking on her door, the door opened and Rebecca, being nicely dressed, was standing in the doorway with a big smile.

"Right on time." she said, looking into my eyes.

"Of course, this is a very special day." I responded with a smile on my face, trying to keep my depression at bay. "Are you ready to hit the road?" I asked as I reached over and gave her a kiss on the cheek.

"Oh yes!" She said as we both made our way to my car. I went over to the passenger side and opened the door for her. We drove for about fifteen minutes until we came to Rebecca's favorite Italian restaurant. Making our way into the restaurant and being seated in a window booth, I ordered a bottle of the best house wine.

"What's the matter, Dave?" She could tell I was not myself. "Did something happen yesterday?" There was no need to hide my thoughts from Rebecca. She was starting to read me like a book.

"I was in the family tree room yesterday and found that photo of my Uncle George at his thirtieth birthday party. Like times before, I was pulled into the photograph. It was a great party and seeing Uncle George and listening to all of his stories was the best. In much the same manner as I told you before, I knew he was killed that night by a hit and run driver. So later during his party, when he left with his girlfriend, Melissa, and another couple, to go to the movie theater, I tagged along. I was hoping to stop him from crossing the street and getting killed, and I did! I diverted the group into a liquor store to buy some candy for the show. When we left the liquor store, we crossed at a corner light and went to see the movie."

"So, you did prevent him from getting killed?" Rebecca asked.

"I did prevent the original death from occurring." I answered.

"So, what happened? Why are you so sad?" She asked with her hands holding mine.

"As I said, we did see the movie, but on the way home, Uncle George and Mellissa were leading the group. I was directly behind them, and the other couple was a short distance behind. We could hear a car racing down the street in the background. It turned sharply at the corner behind us as the driver lost control of his car, zigzagging in the direction of Uncle George, Mellissa, and me. Uncle George quickly pushed Mellissa and me aside and we landed on the front lawn of a house. Uncle

George was hit directly, flying into the air, and landing on a driveway two houses down from us. The other couple, having witnessed the accident, knocked on a nearby house and was able to call for an ambulance. Mellissa and I ran over to Uncle George, and we were holding his hands. The ambulance arrived, but it was too late. Uncle George had passed away there on that driveway. The car that hit him raced away down the street, out of sight. I saved Uncle George only to see him die in a different hit and run scenario. I thought I could change history, but I couldn't. It appears you can't cheat one's fate."

"Dave, I am so sorry." Rebecca said as she was rubbing my hands. "Is there anything I can do?" She asked.

"Not really." I replied. "It was just going from a high of saving Uncle George to a quick drop when I saw him killed in front of me."

"I am there for you whenever you want to talk about it."

"Thank you, my sweet Rebecca." I paused for a few minutes and then looked into her eyes and produced my best smile, I said. "Enough of this. Today is your birthday and that is where my attention is going to be at. Why don't you give your mom a call and tell her we are going to stop by. Besides, did you tell me you have something to dig up today?" Actually, she never mentioned the time capsule, but I wanted to have her think she did at some point mention the capsule to me.

"You are right! I forgot all about it! Wait a minute; I don't remember telling you about the time capsule."

"Well, you did. How else would I have known about it?" I said looking at her confusion. That confused look quickly changed.

"You know I should call some of the people that were there at my party and invite them over for the revealing.  I'm going to call mom and tell her our plans." Rebecca was on the phone with her mom going over the details. "Mom said some people have already contacted her regarding the opening of the time capsule. We are setting the party for six o'clock tonight. Mom is going ahead and order a few pizzas for everyone."

"That sounds like fun." I said as our luncheon arrived at the table. "What do you remember about your eighth birthday?"

"Not much. There were different party games and then the cake and ice cream. That was fifty years ago Dave. I sometimes can't remember what happened last week!" We both laughed as we started to work on the food at the table.

Time went by quickly. After lunch we went downtown window shopping, holding hands the whole time. We arrived at her mother's house about five-thirty. As we walked towards the front door, I spied the sign Rebecca's father had placed in the ground, over the time capsule, *This time capsule was buried on Rebecca's Eighth birthday and should remain buried for a period of fifty years.* The guests started arriving a little after six o'clock. All were very happy to get together after so long of a period. Many had not seen Rebecca for several years. Rebecca's mom had baked a cake which was going to be enjoyed later that night. With the party commencing and time being spent, catching up on lost time, Rebecca announced that we all were going to dig up the time capsule before it got too dark.

A couple of the men, including myself, got shovels and started the process of uncovering the hidden vessel. After the metal box was revealed, the men extracted it out of its cavity, placed it on the grass, and hosed off the years of dirt caked on the outside of the capsule. It was then dried off and moved to the kitchen table inside the house. The party participants formed a circle around the table. Rebecca did the honors of opening the container and started bringing the different items out from its fifty-year captivity.

A doll was revealed, then a baseball card, followed by a newspaper from the date fifty years prior. More toys made their way out of the metal box as the gathered guests had comments and stories on each item extracted. Finally, Rebecca pulled out a note addressed to her. While the other party goers marveled over the removed items, Rebecca, with note in hand, turned away from the crowd and quietly went into the front room, I followed. She opened the note and read it silently to herself.

*My dearest Rebecca, you were only eight years old when I put the note into the time capsule, and now you are just a little older finding the note, I was there at both events. I just wanted to say that I have fallen deeply in love with you and I know you feel the same. You are my everything; now and forever.*

*Love always, Dave*

She looked up from the note and into my eyes.

"I know it's strange and hard for you to believe it, even with what you and I have been through recently, but I really was there at your eighth birthday party. That is why I asked for your photograph that was taken on that day. I used it and got pulled into your birthday event. I was there as everyone sang Happy Birthday to you. I talked your dad into the idea of the time capsule and was able to place the note into the box prior to it being buried. I was hoping that all the things I had told you previously you could now really believe." I said all this holding Rebecca's hands and looking deep into her beautiful eyes. I waited for what seemed a lifetime, but finally she did speak.

"Dave, I too have fallen deeply in love with you and yes, I have come to believe, not really understanding how, but I do believe you can get pulled into photos and experience that segment of time. Yes, you must have been at my eighth birthday and placed that note into the time capsule, there is no other explanation."

We hugged and kissed for a very long time and then finally we returned to the kitchen, rejoining the other birthday guests. All is as it should be.

# XIV

Dave and Rebecca dated another five months before, on one sunset night; Dave dropped to one knee and asked Rebecca to marry him. With tears in her eyes, she said 'YES'. They were married the following year.

The adventurous traveling into the past via photographs, that of Dave's first wife, Helen, on their honeymoon in Hawaii; the civil war solider, Jimmy Bob Lansford; the photograph of Rebecca's eight birthday party; and finally, the snapshot of Dave's Uncle George's thirtieth birthday party, where he was able to visit with his uncle one last time; these were the last. All future attempts to be drawn into photographs seemed to have stopped. Dave was fine with that, he now enjoyed spending time looking to the future with Rebecca and less time working with the faces from the past.